Yitz Berg from Pittsburgh

Volume 1

Yitzy and the G.O.L.E.M

By Sholom Cohen

Yitz Berg from Pittsburgh
Yitzy and the G.O.L.E.M

First Edition
First Impression-November 1992
Published by Jewish Reader Press

ISBN#0-922613-50-8

Distributed by
Hachai Publishing
156 Chester Ave.
Brooklyn, New York 11218
(718) 633-0100

Typesetting by
Mendelsohn Press
Tel. (718) 467-1957
Fax. (718) 778-5918

Contents

Chapter 1

The Game

"Come on, Yitzy. Make him jump! Make him jump!" "I am, Moishy. He's going up to the next level, now," Yitzy answered, as he piloted the Mendy figure on the computer screen. "Watch me now, and I'll pick up some sparks."

"Hi, Moishy," called Moishy's five-year-old sister Chaya, as she walked into her brother's room, disturbing their concentration on the game. "Mommy says to put the game away and start your homework," she said in her sassiest voice.

"We can't stop now," Moishy said. "Yitzy almost has the golem released."

Chaya skipped over to the computer to watch the action on the screen. "What's a golem?" she asked, as she saw Yitzy moving the figure up a series of hills.

1

Moishy pointed to a robot-like creature at the top of mountain. "Haven't you ever heard of *Mendy and the Golem*?" Moishy asked. He pulled Chaya's ponytail and grinned at her. "How would you like me to read it to you for a bedtime story?"

"Oh, goody!" Chaya said. "But just tell me now, who's Sholem and what's a golem?"

"It's from the book," Moishy answered. "Mendy's a kid who has a pet golem named Sholem." As Chaya watched, Moishy explained that Sholem was like the giant robot that rescued Jews from bandits during the Middle Ages. In the game, the evil Dr. Hardheart has kidnapped Sholem the golem, and is using Oy Vayder, another golem, to hold Sholem captive. "Yitzy's guiding Mendy up the hills to free Sholem," Moishy finally said.

Chaya and Moishy both watched as Yitzy held the joystick loosely in the palm of his hand. He gently pushed the stick forward, backward, or side-to-side to move Mendy and pressed the stick's button to make him jump. Mendy was now at the top level, ready to use a spark to break one of the chains that held Sholem. Yitzy pressed the button to lift Mendy up to the ladder that would carry him up to use the sparks to free Sholem.

"Watch out, Yitzy! Dr. Hardheart's sending the rocks down to get you, "Moishy called out.

"Don't worry, Moishy. One more step up this ladder and ..."

"Hey, easy on the joystick. I used my *Afikomen gelt* to buy it, "Moishy called out as Yitzy nearly tore the stick loose. Yitzy tried to bring Mendy down the ladder as he was peppered with rocks thrown down by Dr. Hardheart.

He had to get safely down to the bottom level one more time, pick up another spark, and get back up to break Sholem's last chain. This was the third day they had been playing "*Mendy and the Golem*", but though Moishy and Yitzy were both expert video game players, this was the first time either had three of the four chains free.

Now, Yitzy was heading back up the hills to Sholem. He was about to pick up one more spark, jumping to retrieve it as another rock came down on him. "Oh, no," Yitzy cried, "I've gotta stay up long enough to grab the spark and jump over the rock." But as he came down with the last spark, the last one needed to free Sholem, Yitzy let Mendy be struck by the rock. Yitzy banged the joystick to the side, fell back in his seat, and let out a deep sigh.

"Heh, heh," the synthesized voice of Dr. Hardheart called out from the computer, "I've beaten you again."

"Aw, Yitzy," Moishy said. "You had it beat, and you let yourself get struck by a rock. You jumped too soon."

"Can I play?" asked Chaya.

"Maybe later," said Moishy, "after Yitzy and I are finished; okay?"

Yitzy pushed the joystick to Moishy. "It's your turn, wise guy; let's see you beat my score. It's the best we've had so far."

"No, that was the last game," Moishy replied, as he pulled out the game disk and rebooted the machine. "I've got homework — that essay for Rabbi Lantzman. Did you forget, it's due tomorrow?"

Yitzy had been working on the essay for days, knowing that the best essay would win extra credit and a secret award from Rabbi Lantzman. "I've been working real hard on mine. I want to win Rabbi Lantzman's prize."

"You and me both," Moishy answered. "Do you want to work on it together?"

Yitzy didn't want Moishy to know how much time he had put in on his essay, so he thought he'd better not say it was almost finished. "I think I'd better head home," Yitzy said. "I have some other work to do besides the essay. Thanks for letting me play your game, though. It's great."

"Anytime, Yitzy. See you in school tomorrow." Moishy watched Yitzy leave his room and pulled out his notebook to start his assignment.

Chapter 2

The Essay

Mrs. Berg was coming down the steps to the living room, as Yitzy walked in. He was about to throw his backpack and coat on the floor, when his mother caught him. "Is that where your things go, Yitzy? Let's see. It seems you promised to take those up to your room, or lose mitzvah points."

Yitzy needed every point he could get to trade in for his own copy of *"Mendy and the Golem."* But the corner of the living room seemed like such a good spot for his school things. "Aw, come on, Mom. I just want to leave them here till I grab something to drink. Can't I leave them here for just a minute?"

"Take them up to your room," his mother ordered. "You can have something to drink after they're where they belong."

Yitzy trudged up the two flights of stairs to the attic bedroom he shared with his older brother, Dovid. Throwing his things down on his bed, Yitzy was about to head back downstairs when he decided to take out his essay and read it over, one more time. He knew there were still a few things he wanted to change. He was proud of the work he had done, and though he heard his brothers' voices streaming in the back window where they were playing outside, he started to work on the final part of his assignment.

Yitzy knew Rabbi Lantzman would like his work. He had spent extra time with his father reviewing the *Gemara* they had been learning in school to make sure he understood the discussion between the commentaries. Now he hoped he had explained it well enough to win the best essay award.

Rabbi Lantzman was Yitzy's favorite teacher at the Shevas Achim Torah Academy, so it meant a lot to Yitzy to win the prize. Not only was Rabbi Lantzman a good teacher, but he also had helped Yitzy through his first difficult days in the new school. Yitzy had moved to Pittsburgh from the Midwest in the middle of the year, and that was hard enough. All the other kids in the class knew each other, and it was tough breaking in. But when they starting calling him "Yitz Berg, from Pittsburgh" in that sickening sing-song, he was ready to turn around and head back west. Rabbi Lantzman had come to Yitzy's defense, though, with one of his famous stories. And somehow, Yitzy survived those first few weeks.

This school was also much different. The boys and girls went to school in different buildings. This was the way many of the Jewish schools were in New York, but it came as a surprise that Yitzy and his brothers would go to one school and his sisters to another. He also wasn't used to walking to school every day. Where he had come from, the community was spread out so there were buses and car-pools. But Pittsburgh had a very centralized Jewish community, mostly in the Squirrel Hill neighborhood, so almost everyone could walk. Yitzy had moved to Pittsburgh in the middle of winter, so he had to get used to the cold, early morning walk to school, and the walk home in the early evening darkness.

By far the most difficult challenge for Yitzy was picking up *Gemara*. The topic seemed to have no practical meaning. It dealt with questions of damages a sheep or other farm animal caused when the animal's owner was careless. There were all kinds of special cases if the animal was thirsty, or left out in the sun, or was known to be wild. Of course, Yitzy realized that these were laws from Mt. Sinai, just like *Shabbos* and giving charity, but he'd probably never own a sheep or a bull. Why did he have to worry about the damages they could cause? Then, there was the whole new set of subjects he had to learn. The language, an odd mix of Hebrew and Aramaic, was hard enough, but there were no vowels, no punctuation, and funny abbreviations. It was hard enough to get through the simple reading of a page. He also had to take apart a *Gemara*—case, questions, solution—and deal with all the dead ends in the discussion. It may have been easy for the rabbis but it was a lot for a twelve year old to understand.

Maybe that was the other reason he wanted the award so much. When he came into class in the winter, he was behind the other boys, and had to work hard to catch up.

Rabbi Lantzman had encouraged him, helping him open up, and teaching him a new understanding of the words from *Pirkei Avos*: "Someone who is bashful cannot learn." So stumbling at first, and even falling a few times, Yitzy began to catch on, and now he was up to the others in his class. He sometimes even helped his learning partner, Moishy, cover some of the difficult parts of the Gemara.

With Rabbi Lantzman's help and encouragement, and four months of Yitzy's hard work, Yitzy was fully a part of his class. His nickname was as much a part of him now as was the crooked way he wore his yarmulke, lopsided just above his left ear. That had been his trademark at his other school in Missouri, in fact, but now he was Yitz Berg from Pittsburgh, and he almost enjoyed the name. But if anyone used that sing-song, he'd let 'em have it.

Yitzy couldn't imagine what the prize could be—maybe a new book, some Rebbe cards, some tickets to a Pirates game. But the biggest prize of all would be giving his teacher and friend some *nachas*, by showing how much progress he had made.

Yitzy had completely lost track of the time, when his mother called up, "Yitzy, time for dinner." He ran downstairs to eat, but his mind was on finishing his assignment that night.

Chapter 3

The Final Product

Yitzy jumped out of bed when his alarm went off the next morning. He couldn't remember a morning when he had looked forward to school so much. He said his morning prayers with special feeling before dashing downstairs for breakfast.

Yitzy rounded the corner at the bottom of the stairs at the entranceway of the house. He barreled into his father who was just coming in the door, having just returned from shul.

"You look like you were just shot out of a cannon," Dr. Berg said, as he set down his *talis* and *tefillin*. "What's the rush? Do you have an early morning baseball game?"

"No, Ta," Yitzy replied. "I'm just anxious to get on my way to school this morning."

Yitzy's mother had just finished feeding the baby when

Yitzy and Dr. Berg walked into the kitchen. "Aviva," Dr. Berg said to his wife, "are you sure this is the same Yitzy that had to be schlepped bodily out of bed every morning to get him to school on time for the first three months we were here? "Dr. Berg poured himself a cup of coffee and joined his wife at the breakfast table. "We'd better put a safety belt on him while he eats breakfast or he might jump right out of his seat."

"I'm just excited this morning because I'm planning to turn in an assignment today," Yitzy explained. Yitzy's father was always doing assignments and making presentations. "Haven't you ever been excited about turning in an assignment?" "Well, that depends," his father said. "Depends on what?" Yitzy asked. "It depends on what I'm turning in," his father said, "and who's getting it." Yitzy thought about that. "Well, I'm pretty happy with what I'm turning in, and I'm giving it to my favorite teacher."

"Rabbi Lantzman?" asked Dr. Berg, as he looked at his wife.

"Who else", replied Yitzy. "And if he likes it, I'll win the best essay award."

Mrs. Berg smiled at Yitzy's answer. She and Yitzy's father had met with Rabbi Lantzman several times to see what they could do to help his adjustment to the new school. Somehow, neither his older brother nor his younger brothers and sisters had any problems in the school during their first year, but probably because of the new challenge of Talmud, Yitzy felt unprepared. Both of Yitzy's parents agreed that Rabbi Lantzman had made the difference in getting Yitzy to feel comfortable in the new school.

"Yitzy," Dr. Berg asked, "were you using the computer

last night to work on your essay?" "I was putting on some finishing touches," Yitzy answered as he poured himself some cereal. "Do you, by any chance, know what happened to the disk I was using?" Dr. Berg questioned.

"What disk was that?" Yitzy replied nervously.

"I guess it was the one you used to write your report on," said Yitzy's father, realizing that Yitzy was responsible for his lost disk.

"I didn't use it write the report," Yitzy said. "I just wanted to make sure I had an extra copy in case anything happened to the original."

Yitzy's father agreed that was a good idea. "You should check before you use someone else's property," Dr. Berg continued. "I need that disk at work, so you'd better return it to me before you go to school."

"You're taking it to work?" Yitzy asked with a certain glow. "That's even better. In case the house burns down, you'll have my extra copy safe and sound at your office."

"G-d forbid," Yitzy's mother interrupted. "Don't even say such a thing."

While Dr. Berg was finding out about his missing disk, Yitzy's two younger brothers had joined Yitzy and his parents at breakfast. Yitzy's brother Shmuly was in the class behind Yitzy. He had become a top performer in his class right away, and never forgot to remind Yitzy about it.

"You know, Yitzy," Shmuly said, "you can't be too disappointed if you don't win the essay contest. Remember, the other boys have had a year's jump on you."

"I think you may be surprised," Dr. Berg answered. "Yitzy's teacher keeps telling me he's made unbelievable progress in the last few months. I think it was just a case of shyness. Once he started participating in class, he picked right up," Yitzy's father said.

"Yeah, Shmuly," Yitzy said. "Who said you know it all? What ever happened to confidence?"

"You're right, you're right," Shmuly said, "but there are some pretty smart guys in your class."

"Okay, boys," their mother said. "Let's finish up and get off to school."

"What do you want to bet I do win the award?" Yitzy asked Shmuly.

"I'll show you how much confidence you have," Shmuly answered. "I'll bet any of my computer games against one of yours. How's that?"

"That's enough," their father said. "Writing a *dvar Torah* is not something we make bets on that way."

"What do you mean there's no gambling in the Torah," Yitzy asked. "Haven't you ever heard of the *aleph bet*?"

Everyone in the kitchen let out a loud groan. "That was the worst pun I've ever heard," said Shmuly. "If you write essays the way you make up puns, you'll be lucky if you don't win an award for the worst essay."

Yitzy started to lunge at Shmuly when he looked up at the clock. "Oh, no. I've gotta run or I'll be late for *minyan*. So long, Mom. Bye, Ta. You better watch it, Shmuly."

"Don't forget to leave me that disk," Dr. Berg called after Yitzy.

"Okay, Ta," Yitzy answered. "I'll leave it on the dining room table."

"I've gotta go, too," said Shmuly, as he ran out of the kitchen.

"I hope he won't be too disappointed if he doesn't win,"

said Yitzy's father after his sons had left.

"Not win," said Mrs. Berg. "What ever happened to confidence?" They both laughed as Yitzy's mother did her best imitation of her son.

Chapter 4

Father-Son Softball

A week later, Yitzy left his house one bright spring morning, heading for school. He had forgotten about the essay contest. As Yitzy walked down the stairway that ran from his house to the sidewalk below, all he could think about was the big Shevas Achim softball game. The Father-Son game had become a Memorial Day tradition in Pittsburgh, though it was usually played by fathers whose children were too young to play baseball and by sons whose fathers had already retired from the diamond. Yitzy's big brother Dovid, would be on the team for the first time, and Yitzy had hopes of being allowed to play with the big boys in high school.

He turned off his street to walk up Murray Avenue, and, as always, he was struck by the variety of sights, sounds and smells that it held. In the mornings, as he walked to school, there were stores opening; crowded, rush-hour buses straining their way up the steep Murray Avenue hill; and, along with him, children of all ages heading for school. On the return trip home in the afternoon, most of the stores had closed, but the many restaurants that dotted this part of Squirrel Hill filled the air with a mix of tantalizing smells. Even if he couldn't eat at most of the restaurants, the aromas that wafted from the Greek and Italian fast food shops, the delicatessens, and, of course, his favorite kosher places, kept his nostrils perked up.

This morning, as he passed Joe's Kosher Food mart, Joe was busily unloading what looked like tiny sides of beef. *How can we possibly eat meat from such tiny calves?* Yitzy thought to himself. The thought passed as Joe spotted Yitzy coming up the street, and called out to him.

"Yitzy Berg," Joe said. "How's my favorite catcher?" Joe was sponsoring and coaching a team in the little league that Yitzy was trying out for. Joe was a coach who really knew how to get the most out of "his boys."

"Hi, Joe," Yitzy answered. "Are you going to be at the game next week?"

"Are you kidding?" Joe replied. "I haven't missed the Memorial Day game since, let me see ..." Joe paused. "Well, I guess I can't remember a Memorial Day when I wasn't out in the field or coaching my boys."

"Do you think I'll be able to play, Joe?" Yitzy asked, hopefully.

Joe thought about Yitzy's good play behind the plate, but also about his small size. "You know," Joe said, "we should have a second game for the younger kids, and us old fogies. It's funny, when you're a teenager, you push aside anyone younger, and when you're twenty-five, or so you push aside anyone who's older. Maybe we should have a Grandfather-Grandson game this year, too."

Yitzy didn't quite understand what Joe was talking about, but he liked Joe's idea for a new game. "That would be fine with me," Yitzy told Joe, as he looked up into the truck where Joe was standing.

"Since I make the announcements in shul on Shabbos, I guess I can throw an extra one in about the game," Joe thought out loud. "Well, Yitzy, I'd better get back to work."

"And I'd better get off to school," Yitzy said. "See you later, Joe."

"Have a good day, Yitzy," Joe said. "And remember to keep your catcher's mask on."

That last comment reminded Yitzy of a near disaster in the game on Sunday.

A player had fouled off a ball right into Yitzy's face, knocking the mask off over his head. Yitzy didn't want to think what would have happened if he hadn't been wearing a mask.

Yitzy's thoughts were interrupted by Moishy coming down his block onto Murray. Yitzy ran ahead to catch up. "Do you think the big guys will let us play in the game next week?" Yitzy asked.

Although this was Yitzy's first Memorial Day in town, Moishy was a veteran of the games. He was old enough to remember when they had been fun games, and everybody had a chance to play. Now, the games were played for real, and if you couldn't stop a line drive, or throw from third to first, you weren't even allowed on the field.

"I think we'll be warming the bench all day, Yitzy,"

Moishy advised his friend. "But if the big guys are in a generous mood, they may let us run after the foul balls."

Yitzy remembered what Joe, the butcher, had told him. "Joe says he's going to make a second game for the younger kids. How does that sound?"

"Well, if he can arrange it, I'm in," Moishy answered enthusiastically. "Say, do think Rabbi Lantzman will ever give us back our essays?"

Our essays, Yitzy thought. "Wow, I'd almost forgotten. It's been over a week since we turned them in. What do you think the award will be?" he said.

"Probably some dopey certificate, signed by the principal," complained Moishy.

"Yeah, they always build things up," Yitzy agreed. "Just once, I'd like to see them give out a real prize."

They had just reached the school when Rabbi Lantzman ran up behind them. "Good morning, boys," he called, as he darted by and ran into the school. "Ready to find out about our essay award winner?"

Suddenly, all thoughts of baseball disappeared, and their complaints about past awards stopped. All they could think of was the surprise in store for the winner.

Chapter 5

Decision Day

When Yitzy and Moishy entered the classroom, Rabbi Lantzman was already seated behind his desk. He was reading some loose, typed and handwritten pages.

Were they the essays?

As the other boys came into the class they took their seats. As always, the class was noisy first thing in the morning, and since it was spring, the talk quickly turned to baseball. "How about those Pirates?" Chaim called out to the class. "Still in first place."

"Yeah, what a game yesterday," answered Moishy. "Did you hear that final out?" he continued, as he began imitating an outfielder fading back for a catch.

Adding drama to Moishy's actions, Chaim offered a play-by-play. Now they had Rabbi Lantzman's attention as well, following yesterday's game. "Van Slyke goes back, back," Chaim announced. "He's at the warning track. At the wall. His glove is up. He leaps and makes an unbelievable catch." Right on cue, Moishy collapsed on the floor, with the imaginary ball snagged in his imaginary glove. "The Pirates win the game," shouted Chaim, "and there was no doubt about it!" Chaim's final remarks being the signature of the Pirates' announcer.

They had almost forgotten Rabbi Lantzman was in class. "Okay, boys, if you can tear yourselves away from your instant replay, I'd like to begin."

The Rabbi walked around in front of his desk, and started to laugh to himself.

"I heard a great story," he began, as the boys, knowing what was in store for them now began looking back and forth at each other, in expectation. Here comes another one of Rabbi Lantzman's famous stories.

"You see," Rabbi Lantzman picked up his joke, "there were these two ladies ..."

"What were their names?" someone interrupted from the back.

"There were these two ladies," he started again, "Mrs. Schwartz and Mrs. Friedman. They were sitting in front of their apartment one day."

"Where was the apartment?" another student called out.

"They were sitting in front of their apartment in Miami," the Rabbi continued, as he played along with the game that always accompanied his stories.

"Anyway, Mrs. Schwartz was reading a letter, as she asked Mrs. Friedman, 'Do you remember my son Harvey, the radiologist? You should see what my son writes here.

He says he just sold the car his father and I bought him when he graduated medical school and has bought a new car—a jet black Porsche. Imagine that, my son Harvey with his own Porsche.'

"So, nu, what's so great about that?' replies Mrs. Friedman, not to be outdone. 'My son also has a Porsche!'

" 'Your son?' asks Mrs. Schwartz, 'The school teacher?'" the rabbi continued, trying to imitate Mrs. Schwartz's scorn.

"'In fact,' said Mrs. Friedman, 'my son has two Porsches.'

"This Mrs. Schwartz couldn't believe," continued Rabbi Lantzman, as he started chuckling to himself. "'How could your son afford two Porsches.'

"'I'm telling you,' said Mrs. Friedman, 'he's got two Porsches. A back Porsche and a front Porsche.'" With that, Rabbi Lantzman started laughing uncontrollably. "The laughter started slowly with one or two of the boys, but it wasn't long before the class was rolling with the loud guffaws that usually followed one of Rabbi Lantzman's stories.

Satisfied that the atmosphere was charged up for the start of the class, Rabbi Lantzman said, "Okay class," "I have an announcement to make." Yitzy and Moishy looked excitedly at each other, knowing the announcement that was about to come. "I have finished reviewing your essays," their teacher continued, "and I must say I was very happy with the results." As Rabbi Lantzman spoke, he scanned the class, pausing to look at each boy individually.

"What really made me happy was that you took the assignment as seriously as you did, and tried to learn something new, to find a new way to look at what we had already learned in class. But," Rabbi Lantzman emphasized,

"I did have to select a 'best' paper, as I had promised, and that was very hard." As the rabbi walked back around his desk, the boy's attention was riveted to him, awaiting the announcement. "So it wasn't an easy decision," he said, picking up the folder that held the papers from his desk, "trying to weigh one paper against another."

As he held the folder in his hand, the rabbi slowly and dramatically opened it. He then pulled out one paper, and put the folder with the rest of the papers back on his desk. "And now for my announcement," Rabbi Lantzman began. "When he came into the class in the middle of the year..."

As Rabbi Lantzman spoke, Yitzy suddenly had a strange feeling. He knew he had won the contest and he began to feel his ears burning.

"... Yitzy was forced to catch up with a class that was at least half a year ahead of him," Rabbi Lantzman said addressing the class. "The beautiful essay he wrote shows us just how well he met this challenge. I think all of us agree that Yitzy has made a real contribution to the class, and when you read his essay ..."

Oh no, they're all going to read my essay! Yitzy thought.

"... you'll see that he is very deserving of this award."

Moishy looked across the aisle at Yitzy and Yitzy could read Moishy's lips as he said, "Way to go!"

"And now for the prize," Rabbi Lantzman said with a smile. "I thought about all the prizes we award in the school certificates, books, and so on, but I wanted to come up with something new. So what I decided was to reward the winner with a special assignment."

"You mean I won and now I have to do more work?" Yitzy blurted out as everyone laughed.

The rabbi tried to quiet the class. "I think you'll find this special assignment to be a lot of fun," he said, "so let me explain." Rabbi Lantzman told the class about the new computer system the school had bought for desk-top publishing. "We want to print our own newsletters, flyers and class materials," he said. "We are now going to publish a monthly newsletter, and for our first issue, I'm going to allow Yitzy to help the office staff."

Yitzy knew all about the new system—everyone had seen the boxes outside the principal's office, but Yitzy never thought he would be allowed to work with it. The school had a computer lab for the students, mostly older machines that weren't very good for much more than class work; they weren't even as good as the Apples and PC's that he and some of his classmates had at home.

"Now all of you will have a chance to work on the newsletter in your regular English class next year," Rabbi Lantzman continued. "We're building that into the curriculum. But we thought it would be helpful to experiment with the idea before the year is over so we can plan for next year." The rabbi explained that Yitzy would be working with him and the office staff to put together the first issue and to see how the English class, could help create future issues. "And as a special award, "Rabbi Lantzman announced, "Yitzy's essay will be appearing in the first issue."

Yitzy was finding it all very hard to believe: working on the newsletter, and with his favorite teacher, and having his essay published, too.

"Yitzy," Rabbi Lantzman said, "I want you to meet me in the principal's office right after lunch to start on the newsletter."

"But that's our English period," Chaim said.

"Yeah, and Mrs. McKay will never let him out of English," said Levi.

The rabbi held up his hand as everyone in the class joined in complaining about their English teacher and the strict way she ran her class. "Actually," Rabbi Lantzman told the class, "I've already made arrangements with Mrs. McKay for Yitzy to be out of her class two or three times over the next few weeks, and she's happy to be participating in our plans. After all," he added, "she'll be working on the newsletter with her entire class next year."

Now, Yitzy really couldn't believe it. To be let out of class with everybody's least favorite teacher was the best part of all. He was looking forward to the days when he wouldn't be conjugating irregular verbs or memorizing vocabulary lists.

"So, Yitzy," Rabbi Lantzman said, "I'll see you after lunch. And now let's hit the *Gemara*. When we finished yesterday, the Gemara was giving us reasons why ..."

But Yitzy could hardly concentrate on the rest of the class as he looked forward to his new assignment.

Chapter 6

The Computer

After lunch, Yitzy and his classmates were gathered in front of Mrs. McKay's English class. Naturally, Yitzy's award was the topic of the day, as Simcha commented, "Boy, Yitzy. You really lucked out. Imagine going two or three days with no English period."

"Yeah," Chaim joined in, "how are you ever going to get through the day without Mrs. McKay?"

"Yes, boys," boasted Yitzy, "it's a tough job, but ..."

"Why congratulations, Yitzy?" asked Mrs. McKay, as Yitzy suddenly looked around to see his English teacher standing right behind him. "What's the tough job you have?"

"Oh," Chaim chimed in, "he was just saying how tough it was going to be to miss your class for a few days."

"Well, Yitzy," said Mrs. McKay, "I wasn't able to understand the content of your essay, but I must say it was very well written. I especially noticed how you correctly conjugated each of the verbs."

"Thank you, Mrs. McKay," Yitzy smiled nervously as he turned to go. "Well, I'd better head down to the office to meet Rabbi Lantzman."

Mrs. McKay called after him to tell him not to worry about missing class. "I'll be sure that one of your classmates brings you your homework."

Yitzy was walking away already, but homework or not, he was glad to be skipping that class. As he walked toward the office, Rabbi Lantzman saw him and called out, "Come on, Yitzy, let's get started."

Yitzy could hardly hide his enthusiasm. He was smiling from ear to ear. As he entered the principal's office, he said hello to Mrs. Fishman, the school secretary. Connected to the office was an inner office used for the copying and fax equipment. Yitzy saw the new computer sitting on a table against the wall of this inner office—a full color workstation, with multiple windows and menus, a mouse and an extended keyboard with a laser printer. Comparing this to the others in the school was like comparing a Maserati to a Pinto. *Imagine playing Mendy and the Golem on this computer. I bet this machine is as powerful as the best systems at the video arcades*, he thought.

Rabbi Lantzman sat down in front of the terminal and brought over a chair for Yitzy. "Why don't you take a seat?" he said to Yitzy, pointing to the chair. "I'll just show you how to get started and then you'll be on your own." The rabbi had already booted the system and it was ready for them to use. "Now, do you know about windows?" Rabbi

Lantzman asked.

Yitzy looked at the screen, as the rabbi spoke to him. Instead of one picture covering the entire screen, Yitzy saw several pictures, each of them called a window. There was a clock, with hands showing the time, and another window the size of a normal terminal screen at the bottom of the display. There was also a small, six-pointed star on the screen, that Rabbi Lantzman could move as he moved the mouse controller. The colors were also something new for Yitzy: the background was a pale sky-blue, the windows were pastel yellow, and the characters and borders, a rich shade of brown. Yitzy wondered how to use the rest of the screen.

"Now, this is a very powerful system, Yitzy," Rabbi Lantzman started, "with lots of different applications. You'll be using just one of the applications, the desk-top publisher package called DTP." The rabbi moved the mouse controller to the left along the table, and as he did the star on the screen also moved to the left, and finally rested on top of the window. As the star moved over the border of the window, the edges of the border lit up and the star changed shape to an arrow. "Once the arrow, or pointer, is over the window you can type into it," the rabbi explained. "Just type DTP and away we'll go."

But before starting the program, the rabbi explained that if he hit a mouse button before the pointer was over the window, a special window would come up, displaying a menu. As he was explaining this, the rabbi move the pointer back off the window. It changed shape back to a star, and the rabbi hit the mouse button bringing up a menu. "If this ever happens, just move the pointer off the menu without hitting the button and the menu will disappear," the rabbi explained.

The rabbi cautioned Yitzy that if he did hit the button he might perform an operation that he didn't want to perform. "You really can't do any harm," he said, "but if you're unsure, just click the button again and you'll undo the operation and be back to normal. Okay?"

Yitzy was quickly getting confused. He definitely wasn't used to having so many things to keep track of when he used a computer, but he thought he understood. "I think it makes sense," Yitzy said, "but if something does go wrong, what should I do?"

The rabbi thought for a minute and then answered, "Oh, there will always be someone in the outer office. You can always ask them for help. They are also being trained on the system," he added. "If all else fails, just leave the computer in whatever state it's in, and I'll try to clear things up when I can."

Rabbi Lantzman reached over to a bookshelf beside the table that the terminal sat on. He pulled down the biggest loose-leaf notebook Yitzy had ever seen. *It must be four inches thick*, he thought. It was already filled with printed pages, with lots of fancy pictures. "This is the user's manual for DTP," the rabbi explained, as he set the notebook down on the table beside the terminal. Yitzy was used to the twenty to thirty page manuals that come with the classroom software, but this was something else. "Most of what's in here, we aren't using yet," Rabbi Lantzman told Yitzy. "In fact, there are DTP options described in the manual that we didn't buy, like color printing." The rabbi went on to tell Yitzy that he would be using only a small portion of the operations described in the manual. "I just wanted you to see how complex this software is, but I'll be showing you just what you need to know in order to run the program. I didn't expect you to learn from the manual."

The rabbi then moved the pointer back to the window and typed "DTP." The star symbol disappeared and the screen began flashing. When the flashing stopped, a new window appeared covering most of the screen with the name DTP at the top. "Now, this is how the screen will look when you enter the program," explained the rabbi. He went on to describe the ability of the system to create a new publication, copy an old one, or edit an existing one. "You'll always be editing an old one from our existing data base," he continued. "Also, you don't have to worry about accidentally changing the wrong publication or starting a new one; the system is protected with passwords. The passwords will allow you to get to the current newsletter only."

As Rabbi Lantzman spoke, he showed Yitzy the next set of instructions. When we create a new publication, we can specify a special form. "We have designed a special layout for the newsletter, and it has already been stored, in the memory.

The rabbi then moved the pointer over the menu and selected edit to edit an existing publication. The next menu listed the publications and the rabbi used the mouse to choose the current newsletter. Yitzy was amazed that all of these operations were done without typing any commands or having to remember any file names. That was one of the hardest things about the software he was familiar with: each one had its own commands and formats. When the rabbi finished making his selections, the window changed to show a picture of the first page of the newsletter, exactly as it would look when it was printed. Yitzy couldn't believe what he was seeing. He was used to typing reports on the computer, but he never was sure what they would look like until they were printed. This system allowed you to see the report as you edited it.

The first lesson continued with a description of how to create headlines and articles. Rabbi Lantzman showed Yitzy how to do these operations and then allowed Yitzy to use the system. After the first hour or so, Yitzy felt like an expert, a real maven.

Chapter 7

The Computer Maven

When he ran into his friends Yitzy was still swept up in the excitement of using the new computer system.

"You should have seen it," Yitzy said as he joined up with the rest of his class who was leaving Mrs. McKay's room. "Color graphics, pull-down windows, pop-up menus." Yitzy's excitement was contagious as the other boys listened. "And right in the middle, Rabbi Lantzman logged into a computer in New York and copied out some files that had all kinds of stuff for the newsletter. We're even going to use a scanner to put pictures in. Boy was it neat!"

"I bet all we'll get to do is just watch," said Chaim.

"Yeah," said Levi, "like when we went on the newspaper tour."

"Well," answered Yitzy, "I really got to use the system.

And I'm going back on Friday to do some more work." The school was dismissed early each Friday in anticipation of Shabbos, but this late in the year, Yitzy still had several free hours before he had to start getting ready.

"Well, you didn't miss much in Mrs. McKay's class," Moishy explained. "Another poem by some lady named Dickinson. Here's the homework."

Yitzy stuffed the page in to his notebook and continued his account of the computer session. "Rabbi Lantzman taught me all the main commands," he said, "but since it's such a user-friendly system, you learn just by working with it."

Looking a little puzzled, Levi asked what Yitzy meant by "user-friendly."

"Don't you know anything about software packages," Yitzy answered rudely.

"Yeah, Levi," Chaim chimed in. "You're barely book literate, much less computer literate."

"Oh, yeah!" Levi answered. "I've always passed all my computer tests."

"Then how come we had to call in the service repair after you forced a thick 3-1/2 inch disk into the 5-1/4 inch drive?" Yitzy said, as he advanced the attack.

"Well, we'll see how smart you guys are next period, when we get to math," Levi argued back. "When was the last time either of you got a 100 on an algebra test?"

"It's just a good thing they don't give us algebra tests on the computer," Yitzy said, "or you'd score a big 0."

Just then, Rabbi Lantzman walked up. "What's all the shouting about, boys?" he said.

"Yitzy's being a showoff 'cause he won the essay contest,"

Levi answered.

"You're just jealous because you don't know how to use the computers," Yitzy said.

"All right," Rabbi Lantzman said. "I'm surprised at your behavior Yitzy. Remember, your getting to use the system is a special privilege. Don't abuse it. And don't use it to bait your friends either."

"But Yitzy's right," said Moishy. "Levi's a total klutz when it comes to computers. You remember what he did to that disk drive."

Rabbi Lantzman smiled as he remembered the service man trying to figure out how anyone could jam the thick disk into the thin disk drive. "Shouldn't you be going to your next class?" the rabbi reminded them.

"Hey, Moishy," Yitzy asked, "can I come over after school and play Mendy and the Golem? I feel like I can finally beat that old Dr. Hardheart."

"Yeah, but not for too long. We've got that English assignment to do", "Moishy answered.

Yitzy barely heard about the English assignment. He was already thinking about the new computer game and his plans for working on the newsletter on Friday.

* * * *

After school, when the boys got to Moishy's house, they immediately ran upstairs to Moishy's room. Somehow, the new game made them forget all about their daily, after-school snack.

"Load up the game," ordered Yitzy, "and let's get started."

"Hey," said Moishy, "who appointed you recreation director?"

"I'm just anxious to get started," Yitzy said, trying to make up for his first remark. "Why don't you take the first game."

Moishy got the game loaded in, took up the joystick and started Mendy up the path to rescue Sholem the Golem. As he guided Mendy up to second level, the first boulder came down. "Step back," Yitzy called out. "Now jump, it's rolling down on you." Then he started to grab for the joystick.

"Watch out," Moishy said, "it's my turn." He pulled the joystick back and directed Mendy back up the hill. Moishy pushed the joystick button to get Mendy to jump and grab a Torah spark so he could release the first of Sholem's four chains. He grabbed the spark and continued up the hill.

As the Mendy figure got up to the top level, the boulders fell faster, but Moishy was able to get the first chain undone and proceed back down to pick up the next spark. "That was close," said Yitzy.

"Yeah, and no thanks to you," said Moishy. "We'll see how you do on your turn."

Moishy was able to get the next two chains undone, but with each successive chain, the boulders fell more often, and he didn't make it back up the hill for the fourth and final chain. He dejectedly handed the joystick over to Yitzy, who immediatcly started the game over again.

Yitzy broke the first two chains very quickly and headed back down for the third try. "I think I've finally got this licked," he told Moishy.

Moishy shook his head. "You say that every time," he replied. "Then, when the rocks start coming, all of sudden you get caught, too."

Yitzy was heading back up for the third time and had already picked up a spark. The boulders were coming down faster and faster with each step, but Yitzy was moving the Mendy figure back and forth to miss the falling rocks and timed his jumps perfectly to step over the ones that were rolling down. "One more level" he called as he headed to the top of the hill.

"You've got it," Moishy cried, as he started to root for Yitzy.

Yitzy popped out of his chair as he broke the next-to-last chain and headed back down to break the fourth and final chain. He headed back up, assaulted with boulders on all sides by Dr. Hardheart, but he moved the joystick and timed his jumps with perfection.

"Three more levels, three more levels, and you've got it!" Moishy yelled.

Yitzy sat mesmerized, concentrating on the screen, as he guided Mendy up the hills. Now, there were two more to go, as he fought the boulder barrage. "I missed the last spark, but I've gotta get this one," he said, "or I'll have to go back down for another one."

He and Moishy watched, as the spark passed over Mendy's head. Yitzy pushed the jump button and grabbed it. All that remained was the last hill and using the spark to break the chain. Yitzy sat on the edge of his chair, dodging boulders and reached the top level. He hit the button, but didn't have the Mendy figure lined up for the jump to break the chain. One more try, he thought. He had to move back now to avoid another boulder, but on the top level all he had to move away from were the falling rocks; they only started rolling on the lower levels. Quickly, he moved the joystick to the right, to move Mendy into line for the final jump. As soon as he had it lined up, he pushed the jump button. He had it timed just right, and he was able to break the final chain.

Yitzy leaped out of his chair. "I knew I had it this time, I knew it." And he started to do a victory dance.

"Make sure you don't spike the joystick," Moishy said half-heartedly.

"I told you I could do it," Yitzy boasted. They both watched as the newly freed Golem gave Mendy a big bear hug.

"Oh, no," the voice of Dr. Hardheart cackled. "You've beaten me. But just wait until next time."

"No, you wait," Yitzy answered the machine. "I've got you now. Let's play another round. Do you want to start?"

"No," answered Moishy, "I'd better start my homework. We've got that new English assignment from Mrs. McKay and some Gemara to *chazer* over."

"Aw, let's load up the game again," Yitzy argued. "Mrs. McKay can wait."

"Maybe she can wait," Moishy answered, "but I've gotta start the homework."

Yitzy thought Moishy was being a spoilsport because Moishy hadn't been the first to win, but he didn't say anything. "What was the English assignment, anyway?" Yitzy asked.

"Oh, we have to read this poem, and describe in our own words what the author is saying," Moishy explained. "She gave us around four questions we have to turn in on Thursday."

"Thursday!" Yitzy exclaimed. "That's four days away."

"Oh, look who's talking," Moishy said. "You're the one who always has his assignments done a week in advance."

"Well, I have bigger things to think about," Yitzy said, referring to his work on the newsletter. "But I guess I'll read through the poem tonight."

Yitzy got his backpack and started out of Moishy's room. "See you tomorrow and thanks again for the game."

Moishy shrugged. "You beat it all right. So long."

* * * *

When Yitzy got home, his mother stopped him at the door. "I hear you have an announcement for us."

"You mean you already heard that I beat Dr. Hardheart in the Mendy video game?" He answered.

"What are you talking about?" his mother said. "Your brother came home and told me you won the essay contest."

"Oh, that," Yitzy said. "I'm getting to help Rabbi Lantzman with the newsletter. It's great."

Yitzy's father entered the door just behind Yitzy. "What's great?" He asked his son.

"Yitzy won the essay contest and he's helping Rabbi Lantzman with the newsletter," Yitzy's mother answered.

"We've got a computer just like the one you use at work," Yitzy explained to his father. "It's a special desktop publishing package with all kinds of special windows and menus. I'm sure you'd enjoy using it."

"I'd enjoy any software that worked," his father answered. "You should see what I have to work with."

"And the neatest part is that we can include all kinds of

graphics," Yitzy said. "We even have direct access to news from a bulletin board service in Brooklyn and we can pick up all kinds of data off the network."

"That's probably the Kessernet," "Did Rabbi Lantzman tell you how to get around the bulletin boards, too?"

"Rabbi Lantzman spent over an hour showing me the system today," Yitzy answered, "and I'm going to spend a couple hours Friday afternoon on my own."

Dr. Berg was a little concerned. "Are you sure one hour is enough training? These editing systems are pretty complex."

"It's a piece-a-cake," Yitzy boasted. "Everything's user friendly. You can't go wrong."

Yitzy threw his backpack into the hall closet and started to head up to his room. "Is dinner starting soon?"

"Just a few minutes," his mother replied. "You left your backpack down here. Don't you have any homework?"

"Nothing due tomorrow," Yitzy replied. "But I've got to plan what I'll be doing for the newsletter."

After Yitzy went to his room, his parents started an "I hope this doesn't all go to his head" conversation. "He'd better not let this newsletter substitute for his regular homework," his mother said.

"I'm sure he's just enjoying his big day," Dr. Berg said. "He'll be back to normal by the middle of the week."

"I hope you're right," Mrs. Berg agreed as they both went into the kitchen to get dinner ready.

Chapter 8

Open Windows

Yitzy didn't forget about his newsletter work, but he did forget about every other assignment he had. The last-minute effort he put into his homework, and his lack of attention in class started becoming noticeable.

"Are you here, today?" Rabbi Lantzman had asked one day, as he interrupted Yitzy's daydreams of the Mendy video game and the newsletter program.

But Friday eventually came and Yitzy entered the school office after classes had ended for the day. "Hi, Yitzy," Mrs. Fishman, the school secretary said. "Rabbi Lantzman said he would be out until around four, but that you should continue your work on the newsletter."

"Are you going to be here?" Yitzy asked.

"If you need any help, I'll be right here," Mrs. Fishman

assured him.

With that, Yitzy walked into the inner office that housed the computer: He noticed Rabbi Lantzman's hat on the chair in front of the computer terminal and carefully picked it up and placed it on the table beside the computer.

The DTP program was already started up and Yitzy selected the edit command to continue working on the newsletter. He had brought in a disk from his home computer that contained his winning essay. He planned to copy the file into the newsletter. He also planned to edit some news items from the Kessernet.

He had been working for about half an hour and successfully copied all of his files. He had just entered the commands to save his work and was ready to start copying the files from the Kessernet. He hit the mouse button to bring up the DTP command menu, not noticing that his pointer was off the newsletter screen. The commands that appeared looked like those for the newsletter and he selected the files command, thinking it was for the Kessernet files.

Yitzy was surprised to see an unfamiliar list of file names instead of the newsletter files he was used to. He knew he was out of the program and was ready to exit the menu when he noticed a familiar file entry:

GOLEM

Hey, he thought, *maybe this system has Mendy and the Golem, just like Moishy's.* He moved the pointer over the file name and released the button to open the file.

Immediately, the menu disappeared and the screen went blank. A small window appeared with the entry:

PLEASE ENTER PASSWORD:

Yitzy tried to decide what the best password would be for the Golem game. *Let's see,* he thought, *when the Maharal brought the Golem of Prague to life, he would write Hashem's holy name on a small paper and place it in the Golem's mouth.*

That's it he thought, and after the password line he typed: Hashem

The system came back with an error message:

INCORRECT. PLEASE ENTER PASSWORD:

Well, he thought again, the Maharal created the golem. *Maybe that's the password.* He immediately typed in the name:

PLEASE ENTER PASSWORD: Maharal

As soon as he entered the password, the screen went blank again. Nothing happened for what seemed like a few minutes. *I better go get Mrs. Fishman,* Yitzy thought, and he started to get up to go to the outer office. Then he noticed the screen coming back to life. Only instead of the normal Mendy and the Golem screen with the comic book figures, the screen displayed a few simple lines:

G. O. L. E. M.

Gabbai's On-Line Electronic Memory

Below it was a menu with several entries:

Aliyahs

Calendar

Yartzeits

Announcements

Exit

Yitzy realized immediately that he had entered a program to plan events for the synagogue not Mendy and the Golem. But without thinking about it, he decided to explore the system for a few minutes. He started with the Calendar. When he selected that entry the system brought up a new menu:

> Events
> Months
> Years
> Names
> Exit

He selected "events," and again saw another menu. This time it listed things like weddings, bar mitzvahs, special activities and so on. He selected "bar mitzvahs" and saw a list of names, including his own. There it was, his bar mitzvah had already been scheduled for a little less than a year away. He decided to look at another part of the system, and chose "Months." The next screen asked for a month and year and allowed him to enter either the Hebrew or the secular date. He tried "Tishrei" and the system immediately switched from this year to next. When he entered the command, the screen again went dark and reappeared in the form of a calendar, showing all the days of Tishrei, the holidays, the candle-lighting times, some anniversaries and even some special events, like the *Simchas Beis ha-Shoeva* during Sukkos.

Yitzy decided to exit the "Calendar" program and selected the "Announcement" program. What came up next was a screen that looked like a sheet of paper with announcements on it. It was for this Shabbos and included some birthdays and even the announcement of the Father-Son baseball game. There wasn't much left to look at, so Yitzy decided to get out of the "Announcement" program. He started to select "Exit" but at the last second, he moved his hand and hit "Edit," instead. The first menu disappeared, and a new menu came up on the screen that made no sense to him. It asked if he wanted to link to "Calendar," "Aliyahs," or "Events." He tried to exit, but was left with the announcement sheet still on the screen.

What should I do now, he thought. He hit the mouse button again, bringing up still another menu: "Add, Delete, Edit." *Oh, there's delete*, he realized. *That should delete this page and put me back to the first menu to "Exit."* He selected Delete, and the screen disappeared for an instant. But it immediately reappeared. *What do I do now? If I go get Mrs. Fishman she'll wonder what I'm doing working on this program, but I've got to exit somehow.* He thought he'd move the pointer off the G.O.L.E.M. screen and try to get a menu there, but when he did, it was the regular menu, not one for the G.O.L.E.M. program.

Yitzy felt himself starting to shake and *shvitz*. I've got to get out of this and back to the newsletter. He looked at the clock. It was nearing 3:30 and Rabbi Lantzman would be back at any moment. He looked back at the announcement page and saw an arrow pointing to the left at the bottom of the window. That looked like something he had seen on Moishy's computer to move back a screen. He moved the pointer to the top of the arrow and hit the button. Immediately a new message came up:

PLEASE CONFIRM TO SAVE AND EXIT: (y or n)

That means to get out; all I have to do is type "y" for yes. He immediately typed the letter "y" and hit return.

Just then he heard Rabbi Lantzman's voice coming from the outer office. He knew he had to leave this program before the rabbi returned. The main G.O.L.E.M. window reappeared and with it a menu that showed "exit". Yitzy was ready to exit when another message appeared:

SAVING UPDATED FILES

Yitzy wondered what that meant. What files was he updating? But he didn't have time to think about it. He chose exit from the main menu and as quickly as he had entered the G.O.L.E.M. program, he exited it.

The DTP screen was still there, and as Rabbi Lantzman entered the room, that was all that he saw. He also saw Yitzy slumping weakly in his chair, staring blankly at the screen.

"Yitzy," the rabbi called to him. "Are you okay?"

Yitzy didn't even notice that Rabbi Lantzman was standing behind him. Suddenly, it registered that the rabbi was there. He bolted up in his chair, nearly jumping up out of it.

"Rabbi L-Lantzman," he mumbled. "What are you doing here?"

"I just wanted to make sure everything was all right," he said, hesitantly. "You know, this is supposed to be fun, but you look exhausted. Are you getting ready to leave?"

Slowly Yitzy's senses were starting to return. *Everything's okay*, he said to himself. "I copied some files and formatted my essay," he answered the rabbi. "Do you want to see it?" He started to enter the newsletter program again, but before he could start, the rabbi placed his hand on Yitzy's arm.

"Not now," the rabbi said to Yitzy. "I think it's time to close up and get ready for Shabbos. I'll look it over on my own."

Yitzy started to gather up his backpack, but before he

could get up he started to slump again. *I hope I didn't mess anything up. How was I supposed to know that G.O.L.E.M stood for the gabbai's shul announcements? Gabbai's On Line Electric Memory. I just thought it was a computer game!*

"Do you want a lift home?" the rabbi asked. "My car is just outside."

"Oh, no," Yitzy said. "I'm all set. I guess I've just been looking at the screen for too long. I'm okay." *How can I ever tell Rabbi Lantzman what I've done? I don't even know what I've done!*

Yitzy started up again and walked slowly through the door to the outer office. "Have a good Shabbos," the Rabbi called to him, but Yitzy didn't answer. Mrs. Fishman also wished him a good Shabbos, but he didn't hear her either, as he left the outer office and walked out into the hallway to head home.

Rabbi Lantzman walked out into the secretary's office. "Was Yitzy okay when he came in?" the rabbi asked Mrs. Fishman.

"He seemed fine to me," she answered. "He's been in there for almost two hours. Maybe he has vertigo terminalis."

"Vertigo what?" the rabbi asked.

"Oh, that's a condition that can come on when you stare at a terminal for too long."

"That's what Yitzy said," the rabbi replied. "Say, I can't find the copy of the announcements you printed off earlier. Do you have an extra one?"

Mrs. Fishman thought for a minute. "I think that was the only one I printed out. Do you want me to print it again? It should still be on the computer."

"That's okay," the rabbi answered. "I'll just print out a copy myself. I want to leave it in the shul on my way home. Are you leaving now? I'll lock up."

Mrs. Fishman turned off her desk lamp and got up to leave. "Thanks, Rabbi Lantzman," she said. "Have a good Shabbos," she called as the rabbi entered the inner office to print out the announcements.

"Good Shabbos, Mrs. Fishman," he said, sitting down to enter his printing request.

Chapter 9

The Rabbi's Apprentice

Yitzy's head was still spinning as he entered his house and slowly dragged himself up the stairs to his room. He dropped his books on the floor, plopped down on his bed and drifted off into an uncomfortable dream-filled sleep.

His dream found him back in school walking into the inner office. There was the copying machine, the fax machine, and the computer. Sitting on the chair in front of the computer was Rabbi Lantzman's hat, just as it had been when he entered the room earlier in the afternoon. Only, instead of putting the hat on the table, Yitzy placed the rabbi's hat on his head and pulled out a gigantic notebook. He started leafing through the pages of the huge notebook and sat down to access the computer.

Just as he had done earlier in the day, Yitzy began by

working on the newsletter. But almost immediately things started going terribly wrong. The screen kept disappearing on him and new screens appearing. He couldn't control it. As he tried to enter data into the computer, new data appeared. If he tried to delete data, it sprang back to life. When he tried to type one line, a different line appeared, and when he erased the incorrect line, retyping it correctly produced all the original errors. And whatever he tried, he couldn't keep new windows from popping up.

Soon the windows were covering the entire screen. They were of every possible color and shape, not the soothing blues and yellows he was used to. Suddenly he saw a new window appear on the screen. It wasn't a computer window, but a real sliding window frame just like he had in his room. Staring at the screen, he saw the window open and felt a powerful wind pulling him out of his chair. Objects from the room started to fly out through the window. He felt the hat being pulled from his head and then he was being pulled with it. He fought back with all his strength, but couldn't resist the force of the wind.

His terror at being sucked into the terminal was only starting. He found himself at the bottom of a steep hill. As he started to climb up the hill he realized he was on Murray Avenue. There was Joe's store and the kosher restaurant next door. As he continued up the hill he turned onto the side street that ran up to Shady Avenue. Another steep hill faced him, and as he climbed, the hill seemed to become steeper and steeper. When he got to the top, he prepared to turn and head down the Shady Avenue hill towards his house, but instead of going down, he was still climbing up. Every time he reached a corner and turned, the street carried him up another hill.

Now as he looked up he saw something dropping beside him. It was a boulder, not a hard rock, but more like the papier-maché boulders they used in plays at school. As he climbed the hill, the boulders kept falling around him and then rolling. When he looked up he was terrified to see a figure chained to the top of the hill. But when he looked closer, he discovered it was Sholem the Golem. And next to Sholem was Mrs. McKay. It was Mrs. McKay who was throwing the boulders down on him. He was trapped in a computer game.

He tried to run, but whichever way he turned the boulders rained down on him. And although they weren't striking him, he couldn't escape them either. Then, in front of him appeared a new window. Only instead of looking at the terminal, he was staring through the window out of the terminal. There, at the controls of the game, sat Rabbi Lantzman, turning the joystick back and forth, pushing Yitzy up or down the hills.

"Help me," Yitzy called out to him, but he realized Rabbi Lantzman couldn't hear him. He was running now, trying to escape the rocks thrown by Mrs. McKay, when one of them struck him. "Stop throwing the rocks, Mrs. McKay," he called. Then another boulder hit, and another. "Rabbi Lantzman," he shouted, "please help me, please."

"Hey, you little jerk, wake up," Yitzy's brother Dovid said as he entered the room, fresh from baseball practice. "You're dreaming."

"Mrs. McKay, stop the boulders," Yitzy screamed, still half asleep.

"That was no boulder," Dovid told him. "That was my

baseball glove. I threw it at you to wake you up. It's time to get up and get ready for Shabbos."

Yitzy sat up suddenly. He was bathed in perspiration and breathing in short gasps. "It was so real, Dovid. I was trapped in a computer game and was trying to escape from Mrs. McKay. I was playing the Mendy and the Golem game, only I was Mendy and Rabbi Lantzman was playing."

Dovid shook his head in disbelief. "That's the wildest dream I've ever heard. Say, are going to get ready or not?" he said as he started to get ready for his shower.

Yitzy was really upset now. He was scared half to death, and all his brother could think of was who was going to shower first. Yitzy picked up Dovid's glove and flung it back at him. "Go ahead and take your stupid shower. You look like you haven't showered in a month."

Laughing, Dovid ducked to get out of the way of the glove, and stuck his tongue out at his little brother. Yitzy just sat on the edge of his bed, staring down at the floor.

Chapter 10

The Bug in the Shul

Shabbos night had been a disaster for Yitzy. He had stayed home from shul, which wasn't unusual, considering the late hour of the *davening* during May. But he hadn't complained when his mother reminded him it was time for bed right after kiddush and *ha-motzi*. Usually, he would have tried to stay up, even on a late Friday night. He hadn't even made a fuss about not getting to say kiddush himself. Everyone noticed how strangely he was behaving after he said *Krias Shema* and headed for bed.

With Yitzy's older sister and brother at schools out of town, Dovid was the oldest of the Berg children still in Pittsburgh. So when Yitzy's parents questioned Yitzy's unusual mood, it was Dovid who had to provide the answers.

"He was acting real strange this afternoon," Dovid said

over the soup course. "I think he was taking a nap when I came in and he was having some real, strange dream."

"He took a nap in the middle of the afternoon?" Mrs. Berg asked. "What did he say about his dream?"

"It was really goofy, Mom," Dovid said. "Something about being trapped in a computer game and Mrs. McKay throwing rocks at him."

"You see, Shlomo," Mrs. Berg said to her husband, "I told you he was getting too wrapped up in that computer business. Now it's giving him nightmares. I think you should talk to him."

Dr. Berg agreed, but didn't know if it was the right time yet. "He's only been working on that program for a few days, Aviva. By next week I'm sure it won't be such a big deal anymore."

"First you said it would be a few days," his wife replied. "Now it's two weeks. If it's causing Yitzy to act so strangely," she said, "I think it's time to talk to him right now."

* * * *

At least Yitzy had no more computer dreams that *Shabbos* night. In fact, he slept so soundly, he wasn't even woken by the sunlight streaming into his room. "Yitzy," his father shouted up to him, "time to get up and get ready for shul."

Yitzy woke up slowly and got dressed for shul. He noticed how late it was and that Dovid had already left, then said his normal morning *brochos*, but when he came downstairs, he didn't stop for his regular *Shabbos* morning *mezonos*. Instead he quietly got ready to leave by himself.

"Wait up, Yitzy," his father called to him. "I stayed home late this morning so we could walk together." Dr. Berg usually went to shul early to do some learning, so it was unusual for them to walk together.

This morning walk gave the father and son a good opportunity to chat. The shul was located about ten minutes from their house, so they had time for a nice, leisurely stroll. But Yitzy was, understandably, not at all in a very leisurely mood. It didn't make for easy conversation.

"How are things going on the newsletter?" Dr. Berg asked his son, as they walked out of the house.

"The newsletter?" Yitzy asked, trying to hide his surprise at the question.

"It was all you were talking about all week and now you don't remember it?" Dr. Berg questioned him.

"Oh, I remember it all right. It's going fine," Yitzy answered.

Maybe he has lost interest already, Dr. Berg thought. "Are you going to be doing any more on work it?" he asked Yitzy.

Yitzy wanted to tell his father what had happened yesterday, but he didn't know how to start. "Not for a while," he answered instead.

You see, Aviva, Dr. Berg thought proudly. *I was right about his losing interest.* "Dovid said you were upset about something yesterday. Did it have to do with the newsletter?"

Now I've got to tell him, Yitzy thought. *I can't lie about it.* "No," he said instead, "it didn't have to do with the newsletter." At least that wasn't a lie.

"He said something about a strange computer game," Dr. Berg continued.

"Oh, that," Yitzy started to feel shaky again. "It was just a funny dream I had about the 'Mendy and the Golem' game."

Dr. Berg, who had a strong dislike for computer games, was well aware of that one. "Oh, that's the one you were saving up to buy, wasn't it?" he said. "It's a big improvement over "Ninja lizards."

"That's 'Ninja turtles,' Ta," Yitzy answered, starting to laugh.

Dr. Berg wished that if he had to use the games for recreation, he could at least learn something from them. All that could be said for the Mendy game was that it was fairly tame.

Dr. Berg started to ask Yitzy about his essay, but they were almost at the shul now. Yitzy still wanted to tell someone about what had happened, but he was afraid to say anything. Seeing his friends as he entered the shul temporarily pushed it from his mind.

Actually, the shul was an extension of the Boys' Division of the Shevas Achim school. Before the addition had been built, they had been *davening* in school rooms. The shul had been added on to give the families at the school and others in the neighborhood a nice place to *daven* on Shabbos and holidays.

At the front of the shul sat the Rav, Rabbi Lieberman, who was also the school's head principal. He usually gave the *drasha* during services, and when Yitzy and his father arrived he was just finishing a Gemara shiur that he led every Shabbos morning. Yitzy and his father made their way to their regular seats just in front of the shulchan, and Dovid, who had been attending Rabbi Lieberman's class joined them. The rest of the members of the shul were also finding their usual places.

"I see you finally woke up, sleepyhead," Dovid greeted his brother.

"No thanks to you," Yitzy argued back. "I asked you to wake me when you got up."

"When was that?" Dovid asked.

Dr. Berg tried to hide his displeasure at the boys' remarks. "At least, save your fighting until we're home. We're in shul now."

Yitzy sat down next to his father and enjoyed sitting up front, as it made it easier to follow the *davening*. Services were taking their normal course this Shabbos. The older Mr. Friedman led the *shacharis*. One of his grandchildren was in Yitzy's class and Yitzy seemed to remember something special about Mr. Friedman for this Shabbos. "Ta, do you know why Mr. Friedman is *davening* at the *amud* today?" Yitzy asked his father.

"I think it's his birthday," Dr. Berg answered.

"That's right," said Yitzy. "I saw his name in the announcements."

"What announcements, Yitzy?" asked Dr. Berg, not knowing what Yitzy was referring to.

Yitzy had forgotten until just now the details of what he had seen on the screens yesterday. It had all been one big jumble then, but now it started to come back. "Just something I saw yesterday in the office," he said. "I'll tell you later."

During the Torah reading, Yitzy noticed something else. Instead of the normal hand-scrawled notes, the gabbai was calling up the aliyah from a neatly printed sheet. That's the print-out from the aliyah program, he thought. The Torah reading went very smoothly, so Yitzy was sure now that whatever he had done on the G.O.L.E.M. program, at least he hadn't done any damage.

After the Torah reading, Rabbi Lieberman would deliver his Shabbos *drasha*. But before the *drasha,* Joe Sherman, Yitzy's baseball coach, would read the weekly announcements - the times for services, *simchas,* and other activities. Joe got up to fulfill his weekly duty, but before he started, he explained some new innovations in the shul.

"With the growth of the shul, we've had to make some changes. I think you may have noticed that we're organized a little differently this Shabbos," he began. "We have a new computer program that prepares the list of *aliyahs,* and the announcements, and will soon be used for the shul calendar.

We all have Rabbi Lantzman to thank for his excellent work."

On hearing his name, several members of the shul gave him a *yasher ko-ach,* as was their custom.

Joe continued with the announcements: "I want to start out by telling you that Mincha this afternoon will be 9:30 and that Shabbos ends at 8:30 this afternoon." When he heard this Rabbi Lantzman started to motion to Joe. Looking down again at his announcements, Joe said, "Well, that's what it says here. I guess you just wanted to make sure everyone was paying attention." That brought some laughter from around the shul.

"Next, we all enjoyed Sam Friedman's *davening* this morning," Joe continued. "We want to wish him a mazel tov on, let's see here, his 57th birthday."

"Hey, Sam," someone said in a loud undertone, "you haven't seen the better side of 60 in over ten years."

"You know," Joe said, looking down at his announcements, "I bet this should have been *75th* birthday."

Yitzy felt a sinking feeling in his stomach. *I didn't touch anything in those announcements. What could have gone wrong?* Rabbi Lantzman was also getting nervous now. Rabbi Lantzman looked at Rabbi Lieberman and then at Joe, but all he could do was shrug.

Joe continued on anyway. "We also want to wish a happy anniversary to Yakov and Chana Greenberg on their wedding anniversary." Joe's voice started to trail off. "Say, Yakov," he said, "wasn't Chana your first wife's name?"

"Yeah," he said, "and after your announcement my second wife will probably divorce me, too."

Things were starting to get totally out of control at this point. Everyone but Yitzy and Rabbi Lantzman was fighting to hold back their laughter. Yitzy and the rabbi both had their heads cradled in their arms, waiting for the next disaster. But Joe, *Baruch Hashem*, did his best to calm everyone. "Now, here's the final announcement, and one I'm sure everyone will enjoy," he continued, skipping over the rest of the page. "After shul this morning, there will be a special kiddush sponsored by Dr. and Mrs. Yossi Siegel in honor of the birth of their daughter Rina."

"Dina," Dr. Siegel whispered in a voice loud enough for everyone to hear.

"Rina Dina," Joe dutifully corrected himself.

"No," Dr. Siegel tried again, "just plain Dina."

"Plain Dina," said Joe. "Well, whatever her name is, I'm sure we all wish the Siegels a mazel tov. And now, I have another announcement. If it weren't *Shabbos*, I'd tear up this sheet. I think we'll go back to scrap paper next week." Joe paused for a moment to let things in the shul settle down. "Now, if we can show proper *derech eretz*, again," he continued, "I will call on Rabbi Lieberman for this morning's *drasha*. Rabbi Lieberman?"

Yitzy had slumped over in his chair. Noticing his son's position, Dr. Berg thought his son was just tired, so he gave him a tiny nudge when Rabbi Lieberman got up to speak. But Yitzy had no attention span left. Rabbi Lantzman also couldn't believe what had happened and was noticeably shaken by the embarrassment.

"Everything is by *hashcacha pratis*," Rabbi Lieberman started. "So it seems appropriate to mention a key point from this week's *parsha*. We are all familiar with the story of the *meraglim*; how Moshe Rabbenu sent out 12 spies, everyone a prince of his tribe, to spy out *Eretz Yisroel*. A close reading of Moshe's charge to the spies shows that, among other things, the spies failed to correctly carry out Moshe's command. He had told them to first spy on and report back on the people, and only afterward to spy out the land. The error of the spies was to spy out the land first, reporting on its beauty, and then to spy on the people who seemed unconquerable. You see, Rabbi Lantzman, even princes of the tribes of Israel can make mistakes and switch around the order of the words."

Both Rabbi Lantzman and Joe had to laugh at the Rabbi Lieberman's timely remarks. But that didn't do too much to lessen the shame each of them felt. As for Yitzy, the Rabbi's speech had no effect. He was just waiting for the next disaster, not knowing what other damage he may have caused.

Chapter 11

Nutty Network

Yitzy only wished that Shabbos would go on forever. He dreaded having to go back to school the next day and face Rabbi Lantzman. Somehow he had to explain to him what he had done, how it was an accident. Should he tell his parents first? Shimmy, his oldest brother, would know waht to do, but he was out-of-town at yeshiva. Maybe he should ask his brother Dovid for advice. *No way, not Dovid*, he thought. But how could he tell Rabbi Lantzman he had broken into the program and changed everything around? But he hadn't changed anything, just looked. All he could think about the rest of Shabbos was the mess he had caused, just for wanting to play a dumb computer game.

After *Shabbos* he decided to call his friend Moishy. Yitzy

tried to explain to him what he had done, but Moishy couldn't understand what had happened either.

"Maybe," Moishy suggested, "you could tell Rabbi Lantzman that you just happened to type G.O.L.E.M. and all of a sudden things just started happening."

"I can't do that," Yitzy replied. "He knows that's not what happened."

"What about if you tell him that the G.O.L.E.M. program was running in another window?"

"That's a possibility," Yitzy said. "But he'll know it wasn't. He set up everything for me."

They talked for a while and finally decided it would be best to try to explain what happened, but to say it was all an accident, and that Yitzy didn't know what had gone wrong. It would be hard, but there was no getting around the truth.

* * * *

While Yitzy wondered how he would face Rabbi Lantzman in the morning, a certain colonel was wondering how he would face his commanding general the next morning. Lt. Col. Paul Adamson of the Missile Defense Command had promised the general a complete report on the computer problems that the command had been experiencing for the previous twenty-four hours. The colonel was relieved that, so far, radar and missile computer systems remained in normal working order. Only the computers used for routine business, such as the computer Adamson was using to prepare his report had been affected. But the problems on the colonel's system were making it impossible for him to finish the report, and he had no way of knowing if the weapon systems wouldn't soon be affected.

Col. Adamson's system suddenly stopped responding altogether. "Sgt. Wolfson," Col. Adamson called across to his assistant, "my system seems to have completely hung up now."

Staff Sergeant Linda Wolfson was the chief operator of the missile command's computer systems. If anyone could solve a problem, it was Sgt. Wolfson. She had recently returned from a command post in Saudi Arabia, and had received a special citation for keeping the computer systems operating there. "I'm having the same problem on my terminal," she replied. "What's showing on your screen?"

"Well," Col. Adamson replied, "here's something maybe you could help with. Do you know anything about the Talmud?"

"The Talmud?" Sgt. Wolfson asked. "Well I may be Jewish, but I'm afraid my Hebrew school didn't get to the Talmud. Why do you suddenly want to know about the Talmud?"

Col. Adamson scratched his head. "Take a look," he said. "It's someone's term paper on the Talmud."

Sgt. Wolfson stepped over to the colonel's screen and started to read the data that appeared in one of the windows. "You're right colonel," she reported. "It's an essay on some topics from the Torah and Talmud by someone named Yitzy."

"I can read it too, Sergeant," replied the colonel angrily. "What I want to know is what it means."

The sergeant returned to her terminal and began entering some commands. Her system was still working, but very slowly. "I want to check what programs are running on your computer, but if what I think is happening is happening, we have a real problem on our hands."

As she typed in her questions to the computer's operating system, Sergeant Wolfson asked the colonel, "Say, didn't we have someone out here a few months ago named Berg?"

"Yeah," the colonel answered, "but it was Shlomo Berg. He's with the Pittsburgh Computer Center. He came here to give a presentation on some of his research there."

Col. Adamson returned to reading the data running by on his screen. "Say, that's odd," the colonel said, "I'm able to read through this file and guess whose name just came up right after the end of that Hebrew paper —Shlomo Berg." He waited a few seconds and continued, "And here's another file coming up with his name on it."

"Well, it would fit," the sergeant said as she waited for her system to respond. "He's an Orthodox Jew and he would certainly know about topics from the Talmud. Maybe Yitzy's one of his children."

Just then, Sgt. Wolfson's screen came to life. "I'm afraid the problem is exactly what I suspected, Colonel. I'm looking at a report on the status of the programs running on your system and on the rest of our internal network."

"Well, Sergeant," the colonel said anxiously. "What is it?"

"We have a virus on the system, Colonel," she answered. "And it is rapidly taking over all the systems on the network."

The colonel paused for a second to reflect on the implication of Sgt. Wolfson's discovery. "What do you think the virus is doing?" he asked.

Sgt. Wolfson explained that a virus is a program that can

copy itself from computer to computer, either by a network or by moving disks between machines. It spreads just like a cold, from one infected computer to another.

"If what you say is true, Sergeant," the colonel said, "then we don't have a virus."

"But, Sir," the sergeant interrupted, "when you have programs running ..."

"No, Sergeant," the colonel ordered, "we don't have a virus. We have an epidemic. Get the Pittsburgh Center on the phone immediately. I don't care what you have to do."

Sgt. Wolfson turned to a directory she kept on her desk and started to reach for a phone.

"And when you get that software guy Berg," the colonel growled, "tell him that if he can't fix this thing, I'm planning to target one of our missiles on him. If he watches CNN he'll know I can put a missile right down his chimney."

*   *   *   *

Back in Pittsburgh, the night nurse in the intensive care unit of the Mt.Sinai hospital was having computer problems of her own. The unit relied heavily on computers to monitor the condition of patients. The computer would report the vital signs, heartbeat, respiration, and blood pressure. The computers were also used to record this information over several hours, so that the doctors could track the progress of patients. Even medical treatment was controlled by computer with oxygen and fluids being adjusted automatically. Without the computers, the unit couldn't function normally. Even early on a Sunday morning, when most of the rest of the hospital was asleep, the intensive care unit was as busy and as critical to its patients as at any other time of the week.

The computers in the unit were operating so slowly this Sunday morning that various alarms were sounding. If the computer didn't get the data it needed from the systems monitoring the patient, it would sound an alarm to alert the nurse that an emergency may have occurred. Then a nurse would check the patient to make sure that he wouldn't be affected by a computer error With the computers functioning improperly, alarms were going off all over the place and the nursing staff was responsible for making sure that these were false alarms. But with so many alarms ringing at once, the nursing staff just couldn't handle all problems.

"Contact the systems people, Jo Anne," Mrs. Meecham, the chief nurse of the unit, called to one of her other nurses. "And see if any other department can spare some staff. We can't handle all these alarms on our own."

As Mrs. Meecham waited for some computer help, she used her staff to check all the patients individually. The computer systems were starting to fail, and their operations slowed to a halt.

"The systems people say that they're having the same problems and can't repair anything now," Jo Anne called to her supervisor. "They're telling me that some mysterious files are clogging the system memory and the terminals are being held up displaying some of these files."

Mrs. Meecham directed two of her nurses to pay close attention to a patient who had just arrived from surgery. Another patient was sent back to the recovery area to lessen the load in intensive care. Somehow, Mrs.Meecham's years of training in emergency room procedures enabled her to manage this emergency, as well. "What kind of files are they talking about?" Mrs. Meecham asked. "All I want to know is how the medical staff is expected to handle this case load without our computer facility. Don't they have a back-up?"

Mrs. Meecham went back to direct some of the new staff who had just arrived from the rest of the hospital, while Jo Anne spoke to the systems people. When she came back to the control station, Mrs. Meecham noticed Jo Anne staring blankly at her computer screen. "Well," Mrs. Meecham said, "can they give us a back-up computer?"

"I'm watching our back-up in operation now," Jo Anne said. "The systems people added it a few minutes ago to relieve the load."

"I noticed things had improved slightly," said Mrs. Meecham. "We've had fewer alarms."

"But look at my screen," Jo Anne said to her. "I've got this strange file and can't erase it. I don't know what to do with it."

They both looked at the screen as the contents of the file scrolled across the screen. "What's all that about sheep and property damage?" Mrs. Meecham asked.

"And who's Yitzy Berg?" Jo Anne added. "His name is on the file. Is this disaster his doing?"

"Mrs. Meecham," one of the nurses called in from beside a patient. "Mr. Brown's pressure is dropping."

"Get Dr. Franklin on the phone," Mrs. Meecham said, referring to the head of medical services. Jo Anne looked up at Mrs. Meecham questioningly. "That's right, I don't care what time it is. Tell her it's a life-or-death emergency. This computer disaster could cost lives if we can't handle the unit on our own without the computer," she said as she ran to check up on the seriously ill patient, "and she has to be here to see we make no mistakes.".

* * * *

"What did you say you read in the sports page?" Fred Hammer, the night sports editor, said over the phone to his chief pressman, Joe Peters.

"It's like I told you," Joe told Fred, "Jack Smith is sittin' here readin' an extera copy of the late edition, when he comes to the story 'bout Barry's home run."

"I know that part," the editor said. "What did he find in the article?"

"I'm tellin' you," Joe continued, "it's right between the big rally in the third inning and Drabek striking out the side in the eighth. Somethin' about some shepherds and their flocks, very pastoral indeed."

Fred scratched his bald scalp in frustration. "Well," he said, "you stopped the presses when you found that, didn't you?"

"Nope," Joe answered, matter-of-factly.

Fred buried his head in his arms. "Why not?" he whimpered.

"Well," answered Joe, "why should we stop the press run for Monday's feature section when the errors were in Sunday's sports section?"

"So you finished the Sunday run," rambled Fred, as he nearly slid from his chair. "Where is it now?"

"Delivered to your door by dawn," Joe sang out the paper's jingle. "The first of the hundred thousand we printed should be hitting the newsstands," he said as he glanced at his watch to check the time, "right about now."

"You mean we have a hundred thousand papers running a story about a shepherd in the middle of the sports page?" the editor demanded.

"Nope," Joe said. "It wasn't a hundred thousand copies."

"Maybe we can pull back the ones that haven't gone yet," Joe thought out loud.

"No, Jack tells me we printed one hundred one thousand and forty-four, less the one Jack pulled out to read," Joe laughed, "and they've all been shipped."

"You're laughing?" Fred asked. "I'm gonna lose my job over this and you're laughing?"

"I guess that's why you're sports editor," Joe said. "You win some, you lose some."

* * * *

Dr. Berg slowly moved his hands to answer the ringing phone. "2:13" read the clock beside his bed. Who would be calling at this time? he wondered. He was surprised to hear Paul Sommers' voice from the Computer Center on the other end of the line. "Paul ,what's up?" Dr. Berg asked.

"Well," Paul said, "your name turned up in connection with an abnormality on the network."

"My name?" Dr. Berg stifled a yawn. "I don't generally deal with those issues. Can't it wait till the morning?"

"Shlomo," Paul said seriously, "we're getting reports from all over the country about problems on the network:

files popping up out of nowhere, systems stopping cold, data being destroyed. A hospital even reported that it's intensive care unit was in danger of losing patients over it's computer problems."

"I understand the S.W.A.T. team is prepared to handle these problems," Dr. Berg said, referring to the Software Abnormality Tracking team that Paul was on-call for this night. "But I have no connection to that."

"That's what I'm getting to, Shlomo," Paul said. "It's your files and some files with the name Yitzy Berg on them that are clogging systems from here to the West Coast."

"My files?" Dr. Berg gulped, suddenly wide awake. "How did my ..."

"That's what we're trying to determine, Sir," Paul said. "I think you'd better get down here and try and find out how you got involved in this virus outbreak."

"Who's there now?" Dr. Berg asked.

Paul told him it was just himself and another system operator. But the S.W.A.T. team leader was coming in and they were expecting a general representing the Missile Defense Command on the first flight in the morning.

Dr. Berg started to get dressed. "I'll be heading over there soon," Dr. Berg said, hanging up the phone.

Mrs. Berg had awakened and heard most of the conversation. She wondered why her husband would have to go in to work in the middle of the night.

"I'm not sure," Dr. Berg answered. "But Yitzy and I are somehow tied into some problems at the Computer Center. The S.W.A.T. team is trying to solve them, and they need me there to help out."

"The S.W.A.T. team," Mrs. Berg joked. "You mean the guys with attack rifles and flak jackets? The Center is being raided by those crazy protesters again, isn't it. But why did they call you, and how does Yitzy get involved in all of this."

"Wait a minute, Aviva," Dr. Berg said. "One question at a time." He went on to explain the network problem and just who the S.W.A.T. team was.

"But that doesn't explain how Yitzy got messed up in all of this," she said.

"I know. The only thing I can think of is that it has something to do with that disk of mine that Yitzy borrowed," Dr. Berg continued. "Don't tell Yitzy about any of this yet, but tell him I have to speak to him as soon as he comes home from school. I should be home by then."

"You'll be gone the rest of the night?" Mrs. Berg said.

"I may be gone longer than that," said Dr. Berg. "If my files somehow caused this, it could be considered a criminal act. I might get a year or two in Leavenworth."

"Come on, Shlomo, they can't suspect that you purposely... "

"Maybe not, Aviva, but it would be a big embarrassment for the Pittsburgh Computer Center if the network managers connect me to this mess. Let's hope it's some crazy mistake," Dr. Berg said as he headed out the bedroom door.

"Call me when you can, after it's a little lighter out, okay?" she said.

"Oh, I'm sure they'll give me one call," he said. "It'll be a toss up between you and my lawyer. Now, get some sleep."

"Oh, sure," she muttered, and eased back on to the pillow, her brow creased with worry.

Chapter 12

Hard Times at the Software Center

W hen Dr. Berg arrived at the Software Center, Hank Jeffries, the normally friendly weekend guard, was wearing a serious look. "Good morning, Dr. Berg," he said. There's sure been a lot of action here tonight."

"I can only imagine," said Dr. Berg as he gave his identification badge to the guard to be logged into the building.

"Can you tell me what's going on?" the guard asked.

Dr. Berg thought for a moment. "I'm not sure, but if you don't know yet, I probably shouldn't say anything."

"Sorry for the delay," the guard said as he waited for the login to complete. "The computer has been very slow this evening. Kind of odd for a Saturday night, don't you think."

"Have you seen anything strange on the computer, besides being slow?" asked Dr. Berg. He noticed the login had finally completed.

"Should I be seeing something strange?" the guard asked, as he handed back Dr. Berg's ID. "Actually, I did see something strange, but not in the computer. I had one of the other guards making rounds on the campus bring me a newspaper. Look at the front page of the sports section right there, in the article on the Bucs."

As Dr. Berg scanned down the page, his eyes bulged out and his jaw dropped. "It's Yitzy's essay," he finally spluttered. "What's going on here?"

"What did you say, Dr. Berg?" the guard asked.

"Oh, ah, nothing," he answered. "Can I take this with me?"

"Sure," the guard said. "I'm done with it if you want to keep it."

"Thanks, Hank," said Dr. Berg. And he headed for the elevators.

* * * *

The S.W.A.T center was a maze of machines and terminals. The wires connecting all the equipment had the look of a bowl of gray and black spaghetti. Paul Sommers, who was manning the center, sat at a desk in the middle of the mess, with a phone at his ear, reading from one terminal and typing at a second. Dr. Berg entered the room and motioned to Paul to get his attention.

Paul took the phone away from his ear for a second. "Thanks for coming in, Shlomo," said Paul. "I'll be with you in just a second."

Dr. Berg took out the sports page the guard had given him and started to read the article again. In spite of himself, he had to laugh as he read his son's Gemara essay placed right in the middle of the sports page.

Paul hung up the phone and stood up slowly from his desk, stretching his arms. "My team has been on this thing since Saturday morning, and I've been at it for about ... " he looked at his watch, "eighteen hours straight. We started to see your name just the last few hours."

"How many reports have you had?" Dr. Berg asked.

"See this print-out?" Paul said as he leafed through a stack of papers.

"Are those the reports?" Dr. Berg asked, as he sat down across the table from Paul.

"Oh no," said Paul. "This is just a list of sites reporting problems, almost 350 and growing by the hour."

"Do you have a report yet from *Pittsburgh Today*?" Dr. Berg asked.

Paul thought for a minute. "You mean the newspaper?" he said. "I haven't seen anything."

"Well, you'd better add it to your list," Dr. Berg answered, as he tossed the sports section on top of Paul's desk, adding to the load of paper already there. "Somehow, a file written by my son got into the computer system at *Pittsburgh Today* and ended up on the sports page."

Paul scratched his head as he began to look at the paper. "So now both you and your son are involved?" Paul asked Dr. Berg.

"That reminds me," Dr. Berg said. "I wanted to bring you a disk of mine with the files that have been popping up all over. Maybe the virus is on that disk. Let me run down to my office to get it."

Dr. Berg got up from his chair and turned towards the door. He started out into the hall when he ran into something huge that made him feel as if a door were closing in his face. He was stunned. When he looked up, he recognized a human shape, but he could barely make out the words that seemed to be coming from his direction.

"Going somewhere?" said the monster of a man, over six-and-a-half feet tall, and almost as wide as the door.

Dr. Berg looked up and saw the giant and a second man next to him, about half the giant's size. Dr. Berg was too shaky to answer, and he looked back into the S.W.A.T. center for some help.

"Oh, I'm sorry," Paul said to Dr. Berg. "I should have warned you that we have two investigators from the Network Security Agency here now. The N.S.A. sent them out this afternoon when this thing started to mushroom."

Dr. Berg looked back at the investigators, thinking they looked more like hit men than computer security agents. "I was just heading back to my office to bring back a disk for Paul to check out. Any problem with that?"

"Okay," said "Mr. Shorty." "Peters will escort you there," he said motioning to the giant. "And my name is Hall, Fred Hall. Be sure you do what Peters tells you."

They never told me back at M.I.T. that the computer profession would be like this, Dr. Berg thought, as he headed back to his office with Peters right behind. Dr. Berg opened the door and turned on the light. On his desk beside his computer terminal was a file box of disks. Opening the box, he found the one with Yitzy's report and started to leave the room, when Peters pulled the disk from his hand. "Hey, what are you doing?" Dr. Berg yelled

"Sorry," Peters replied. "This may be vital evidence. I'd better take the rest of your disks as well. Also, make sure your hard disk files are locked so you can't access them either." Peters took the file box, and waited in the doorway for Dr. Berg to comply with the order.

"What's going on here?" Dr. Berg demanded, as he logged on to his system to carry out Peters' command.

"I thought the S.W.A.T. people had told you," Peters answered. "You're under investigation for tampering with the National Network, NatNet. Anybody connected with this NatNet problem may have committed a federal crime. That includes you and someone named Yitzy Berg as well."

"But this is all some mistake," Dr. Berg said. "That disk probably has some virus that's caused all this mess. I had nothing to do with disrupting the network. And the only thing Yitzy did was copy his file on to the disk."

Peters thought for a moment. Dr. Berg looked up in wonder at the giant. He may look like a refrigerator, but Peters seemed to know exactly what was going on.

"Then maybe it was this Yitzy and not you that caused the mess to kick off," Peters said. "Anyway, we need to check everything out fully, and we have the warrants we need to investigate anything remotely connected with this case."

Dr. Berg was finishing up his commands to lock his disk, when Peters mentioned Yitzy again. "Does this fellow Yitzy know what's been going on? "Peters asked.

"Don't bring my son into this again. I'm sure he had nothing at all to do with it," Dr. Berg said, getting annoyed.

"Your son, eh," said Peters. "Seems there was a similar case a few years ago about a father who didn't know what kinds of tricks his son was up to." Peters was referring to a famous case involving the son of a computer expert who had tied up a computer network for days by sending messages to everyone on the net.

Dr. Berg had completed his operations, as ordered by Peters. He logged off his system and headed back to the S.W.A.T center with Peters. When they arrived back at the S.W.A.T center they found Paul Sommers and Fred Hall staring blankly at a flashing screen. "We think we've traced down the origin of the network problem," Paul said. "It's from a computer connection in New York. The hacker who started the problem calls himself the Golem."

"That's an interesting name," said Dr. Berg.

"Does it mean something to you?" Hall asked.

Dr. Berg explained the story about the Golem of Prague, and its mysterious powers. "There's a computer system in Israel named Golem, in fact," he answered.

"Well, whoever this Golem is, he tapped into NatNet from New York and started a program to clog the network with data files," said Hall. "Now, what we need to determine is where the New York connection is and who has been using it. Also, how they just happened to pick up your files." Mr. Hall's final remark was directed at Dr. Berg, and contained an accusing tone.

Dr. Berg turned to Peters. "Mr. Hall," he said, "your sidekick here seized all my disks and files. If I can have them back, I can give you the disk containing my files and you can test it see if it somehow caused the NatNet problems." He found the right disk and gave the rest back to Peters. "Do you think I can be excused for the night, or day," he said as he looked out the window on one side of the room and saw the sun rising on the horizon.

"We have your number in case we need you," Mr. Hall said. "Stay close to home for the next twenty-four hours in case we have to track you down."

"Don't worry," Dr. Berg said, "I wouldn't think of disappearing on you."

Dr. Berg headed towards the stairway.

"It wouldn't be the first time someone ran out on us," Peters called to Dr. Berg.

Dr. Berg caught Peters last statement as he started down the stairs. He walked past the guard station and out of the building; he was exhausted and scared.

Chapter 13

Disappointment

Dr. Berg arrived home a short time later, still shaking from his meeting with Peters and Hall. Dr. Berg saw his son Yitzy coming down the stairs as he entered the house. Between the two of them it was hard to tell who was more upset, Yitzy, over his problems at school, or Yitzy's father with his problems at work. Of course, Dr. Berg didn't know about Yitzy's problems, and Yitzy had no way of knowing what his father had just been through. Could their troubles somehow be related?

"Hi, Ta," Yitzy said to his father. "You look pretty worn out."

Dr. Berg tried to appear as normal as possible. "I was up half the night at work."

"You went into work on a Saturday night?" Yitzy asked in disbelief.

"I had an unexpected emergency," Dr. Berg answered, noticing Yitzy's sleepy appearance. "You look kind of tired yourself."

Trying to cover up his worry, Yitzy answered, "There are some things at school I need to work on today. I'm just not sure what to do."

"Well, don't stay late at school today," Dr. Berg said, thinking Yitzy had some homework assignment to complete. "I'm going upstairs to get a little sleep, now, but I need to talk to you when you get home."

Yitzy wondered what his father wanted to talk with him about. But his more immediate concern was what to tell Rabbi Lantzman, and how to tell it. Of course, he also wondered whether he would survive his teacher's reaction.

* * * *

When Yitzy arrived in class that morning, Rabbi Lantzman was already sitting quietly behind his desk. As Yitzy walked in, the rabbi briefly turned his head to look at him. Yitzy gave a meek smile that the rabbi didn't return. Yitzy saw Moishy and whispered, "He knows."

"How do you know, he knows?" Moishy whispered back.

"I just know he knows," Yitzy said, as he set his books down on his desk. "I can sense it."

"What are you going to do?" Moishy asked.

Yitzy walked back towards Rabbi Lantzman's desk. "I'm going to try to tell him," Yitzy said as he turned on his heels.

When Yitzy got to the rabbi's desk, the rabbi was looking up at him. "Rabbi Lantzman," he said, "could I talk to you for a minute?"

"I think it had better wait until after class," the rabbi said. "It's going to take more than a minute."

How does he know? Yitzy wondered. *Is he reading my mind?*

The half-day Sunday session seemed longer than Yitzy could ever remember. Everyone else was anxious for the shortened day to be over so they could head over to the Colfax school to practice with the high school boys for the Memorial Day baseball game. But Yitzy's mind was turning the events of the last two days over and over, trying to make some sense of them. At least Rabbi Lantzman didn't call on him all day. He wouldn't have been able to present any of the *Gemara* or answer any of the questions, his mind being so preoccupied.

Finally, one o'clock came, and the class was dismissed. Everyone dashed for the door, except Yitzy and Rabbi Lantzman. Yitzy sat in his seat, staring down at the closed *Gemara* on his desk, waiting for everyone else to leave.

He hadn't noticed that Rabbi Lantzman had taken the seat in front of him, until the rabbi gently placed his hand on Yitzy's shoulder. Yitzy jumped, and suddenly all the speeches that had gone through his head for the last day came bursting out.

"It was an accident, Rabbi Lantzman," he said. "I didn't mean for anything to happen. I didn't even know what I was doing. I promise it won't happen again. I know you're mad at me, I'm sorry I ever heard of 'Mendy and the Golem.' "

Now, Rabbi Lantzman didn't know how to start. Was this the same Yitzy who had so proudly accepted his award only a week ago? "You should know, Yitzy," the rabbi started, "that I'm not mad at you. I'm upset about what you did; I'm not upset with you."

"But all I wanted to do was play 'Mendy and the Golem,' Yitzy tried to explain. "I didn't know I was going to cause such a mess with the program."

"That's exactly why I am so upset," the rabbi continued. "You seem to think the most important thing is that you accidentally erased some information. You don't seem to be concerned about the damage you've done to your friends in the shul."

The rabbi was right. Yitzy was so upset about entering the G.O.L.E.M. program without permission that he hadn't even thought about how his playing around had caused so much embarrassment. "But I didn't mean to embarrass anyone. It was all an accident."

"Yitzy," the rabbi said calmly, "do you remember the first *mishnah* we learned together this year, when I was tutoring you?"

I'm sitting here waiting to be expelled, Yitzy thought, *and he wants me to remember some mishnah about sheep and shepherds?*

"I was tutoring you to help you catch up," the rabbi continued. "It was the first *mishnah* of the *perek*."

Yitzy remembered it, all right. He had memorized it along with all the other *mishnayos* in *Baba Kama.* "I remember the *mishnah*," Yitzy said, it's about locking up sheep at night, but I don't understand what that has to do with using a computer."

"You know," Rabbi Lantzman said, "we have a saying: 'It's not enough to master Torah, we have to let Torah master us.' Everything we teach you here can help you be a better person, by better serving G-d, by doing what he wants us to do."

"And G-d even wants us to lock up our sheep at night?" Yitzy said.

"Even that," the rabbi said. "You see, the Torah talks to shepherds because that was such a common business then; many people were farmers and had animals that had to be taken care of . If the animals were allowed to wander freely, they could damage another person's property and belongings. If someone was not careful about tying up the sheep and one escaped because of his carelessness, he was responsible for the damages."

Yitzy knew the *Gemara*, and could even explain the cases and how damages were assessed. "Today, we have other kinds of businesses," the rabbi explained. "But we still must be careful of other people's property and of their feelings, too. If we are not careful and someone gets hurt, we are responsible. For example, to be sure that someone doesn't use the computer improperly, we have passwords to make sure that only certain people can use it. That's like locking up your sheep at night. If you do it carelessly, the wrong person could use the system, and if some damage was to result, you'd be responsible."

Yitzy was starting to understand, but it seemed that Rabbi Lantzman was blaming himself.

"That's the one thing in this puzzle I haven't figured

out," Rabbi Lantzman said. "As soon as Joe finished the announcements, I knew he was reading an old version that had been corrected later. I had printed off a good version earlier in the day, but when I came back to the office I couldn't find it. That's why I came into the computer room when you were there. I printed off a new copy, but didn't bother to read it carefully enough to see that there were some changes."

"But I didn't change anything," Yitzy protested.

"Well, in a way you're right," the rabbi said. "What you did was to erase the good version, and leave an old backup copy." *That's what it meant when the program said it was updating files*, Yitzy thought. "Last night," Rabbi Lantzman explained, "I came back to see how the good copy had been changed, and found some entries in the computer that showed someone had been using the G.O.L.E.M. program after the good announcements had already been prepared. I checked with Mrs. Fishman, and she said the only users of the computer had been you and I. But what I still can't figure out is how you got through the protection without knowing the password."

"Oh, that was the easy part," Yitzy explained. "I figured if the program was called G.O.L.E.M., it would take Hashem's name to start it up. When that didn't work, I tried Maharal, and that's when all this trouble happened."

Rabbi Lantzman brushed his brow with the back of his hand. "You've just proven the first rule of passwords, 'Don't choose a password someone else is likely to guess.' You see, I didn't lock my sheep up properly."

"Now that we know what happened," Yitzy said sheepishly, "can I go now?"

"Hold on there," the rabbi said, "there's enough blame here to spread around. I think you need a second lesson from this *Gemara*. You certainly know we talk about the good and the harmful tendencies we have."

Yitzy nodded.

"And how our tendency to do the wrong thing is controlled by our animal soul," the rabbi stated.

Yitzy nodded again and silently thought about the lessons he had in *tov* and *rah* and the Nefesh Elokis and *Nefash ha-behamis*.

"G-d gives you the choice to do what's right or what's not right," the rabbi continued. "When you don't lock up your animal properly, the part of your soul that runs to do the wrong thing is let free. It's in control, but you are still responsible. You are responsible because you didn't take care to lock it up, to pay attention to what your parents and teachers have taught you so that you could overcome that improper tendency."

"But all I wanted to do was play a computer game," Yitzy said finally.

The rabbi became very stern. "You were told by me not to operate any of the software outside of the newsletter program. You had several opportunities to break out of the G.O.L.E.M. program, but didn't. You also could have told me or Mrs. Fishman what had happened. But you chose to have some fun on the computer, instead.

"Improper use of a computer is very serious. Suppose, instead of deleting a few announcements, you had deleted the entire calendar. Do you know how many hours of work went into setting that up? And although you didn't do any permanent damage to the computer, your actions hurt several people in the shul, including some of your personal friends. And you've hurt me as well."

Rabbi Lantzman paused for a moment while Yitzy sat in complete silence. "But there's another point to remember, something positive," the rabbi said. "When you control your *yetzer ha-rah*, you have so much more energy to do good."

Yitzy thought about how much time he had spent thinking about his improper use of the computer, time he should have spent enjoying Shabbos.

"And now, I have to decide upon some consequence that will reinforce upon you what I've said," the rabbi continued. "Normally, in cases of computer abuse, the punishment involves community service. So I think we'll find some activities that you can volunteer for."

That didn't sound bad at all to Yitzy, who had been expecting his expulsion from school.

"The school has some mailings going out," the rabbi said. "I know tomorrow's a holiday, but the office will be open, so I think you can start tomorrow by coming in to work on the mailing."

"But I was planning to work on the newsletter tomorrow," Yitzy ventured.

"The newsletter?" Rabbi Lantzman questioned. "I think it will be long time before you work on the newsletter again. It will be a long time before any of us do much more with the computer, in fact. I think the mailing will keep you busy most of the morning and early afternoon."

But noon tomorrow is the time for the Father-Son game, Yitzy thought to himself. "Then I'll have to miss the big game tomorrow," Yitzy reminded Rabbi Lantzman.

"I'm afraid that's part of your punishment," the rabbi said. "Be in the office tomorrow around 10 and we'll show you what we want you to do."

Yitzy got up to leave. "Don't look so sad Yitzy," the rabbi said. "Just look at this as an opportunity to improve your understanding of yourself and your behavior."

"It's pretty hard to think about improving anything right now," Yitzy said. "For a while, I think I'll just concentrate on not doing anything else wrong. Do I have to tell my parents about what happened?"

"I'll leave that one up to you," Rabbi Lantzman said, as Yitzy left the classroom and headed home.

Chapter 14

Tied in Knots

"Aviva," Mrs. Berg heard over the phone, "it's Chaya Fishman calling."

"Chaya, how are you?" Mrs. Berg answered, wondering why the principal's secretary was calling. "I haven't spoken to you in weeks. Is something wrong at school?"

"No, not at all, Aviva," Mrs. Fishman replied. "I just want to congratulate Yitzy on seeing his essay published."

"Oh," Mrs. Berg said. "We were thrilled that Rabbi Lantzman had chosen his essay for the school newsletter."

"I'm not talking about that," said Mrs. Fishman. "Didn't you know that the essay was printed in *Pittsburgh Today*?"

Mrs. Berg took the phone away from her ear and stared at it, as if Mrs. Fishman could see her puzzled look. "Did you say in *Pittsburgh Today*?" Mrs. Berg said. "Who published it there?"

Mrs. Fishman described its unexplainable appearance in the middle of the sports page. "You didn't know anything about it?" Mrs. Fishman asked.

"No," Mrs. Berg answered, "but I'll definitely speak to Shlomo about it. Thank you for letting me know," she said as she hung up the phone. "Hm, that's funny," Mrs. Berg thought out loud. "How could that have happened?"

Dr. Berg was coming down the stairs, having just awakened late in the morning after his emergency at work. "How could what have happened?" Dr. Berg asked, catching the end of her phone conversation.

Mrs. Berg told him about Mrs. Fishman's call, and Dr. Berg explained the possible cause of the misplaced essay. He also asked his wife not to give the explanation out until the Computer Center had verified the problem. But the phone at the Berg house continued ringing all morning. By noon, the whole neighborhood had seen Yitzy's essay on the sports page and had phoned to congratulate Dr. and Mrs. Berg on having such a talented son. His report deserved a Pulitzer prize, another of Mrs. Berg's friends had said. Since the Bergs couldn't say anything about the computer problem, they both had to endure the phone calls.

When Yitzy got home his father and mother were waiting for him. Dr. Berg had already explained to his wife more about what was happening at work, and some of it Mrs. Berg had figured out on her own.

Yitzy knew nothing about the sports page or his father's problems. All he knew was that he had violated his teacher's trust and had to accept his punishment. As he walked into the house, the looks on the faces of his parents gave him the same feeling he had felt when he saw Rabbi

Lantzman that morning - they know.

"Hi, Ma, hi,Ta," he said nervously. Trying to avoid the subject he continued, "Is lunch ready, yet?"

"I think lunch can wait for a few minutes," his father said. "I wanted to ask you about the files you copied onto my disk a few weeks ago."

Yitzy thought for a few seconds. Only a few weeks had passed since Yitzy had handed in his essay, but it seemed like a lifetime. "You mean my essay?" he said finally.

"Are you sure that was all that was on that disk?" his father asked.

Yitzy thought he might have been mistaken. Maybe his parents didn't know? Why did they want to know about his essay? "That's all I copied. Why do you ask?"

Yitzy's father took a deep breath. *He seems as worried as I was this morning*, Yitzy thought. "I'm in some trouble at work," his father said. "That disk is the only connection I can make. Somehow your file has been copied to computers all over the country."

Yitzy's father tried to explain the network trouble he had been working on the night before, but Yitzy didn't understand him. Then he mentioned the apparent source of the trouble. "The investigators said it came from someone named the Golem," his father said.

"Oh, no," shrieked Yitzy, "not again. I didn't mean to do it. It just happened. I don't know how." He felt like he was about to cry as he poured out the story for the second time that day.

"What are you talking about?" his father asked. "You're not making sense. Golem is some computer hacker in New York."

Yitzy shook his head back and forth. "No, he's not, he's right here in the computer at school, and I let him out. First he messed up the announcements, then my essay goes to the paper, and now ... I just don't understand."

Yitzy's parents sat staring at each other in disbelief. What was Yitzy saying? His mother went to him, holding him close to her as he started to cry. "It's not you, Yitzy, it's not. It's some virus someone has spread that got hold of your report. Please don't blame yourself."

Mrs. Berg succeeded in calming Yitzy. He and his parents sat quietly for a few minutes. When Dr. Berg sensed that Yitzy could talk again, he asked about the school computer: "What did you say about the computer at school? I didn't understand what you were talking about."

Yitzy started to cry again. "Take your time," his father said, "I just want to understand what's upsetting you."

"I guess Rabbi Lantzman didn't tell you," Yitzy said.

"Rabbi Lantzman?" asked his mother. "Did you talk to him," she asked her husband.

"No Ma," Yitzy said. "If he had told you, this would all make sense. I was using the school computer on Friday, working on the newsletter, when I started to use the G.O.L.E.M. program."

Yitzy's father couldn't believe what he was hearing. His son had started this whole mess from the school office. "How did you get to the network?" his father asked.

Yitzy went on to explain everything he could about what had happened Friday afternoon. "I copied some files from the network," he said. "Maybe I copied my files back to the network without knowing it. I did everything else without knowing it."

Dr. Berg thought about that possibility. He was not an expert on networks but the Kessernet that Yitzy used to copy the files had no connection to the NatNet, at least none Dr. Berg was aware of. And just copying files couldn't set off a massive computer failure. "I think we had better get over to Rabbi Lantzman," Dr. Berg said. "Maybe he can help us solve this problem."

Dr. Berg and Yitzy got up to leave. "We'll see you later, Aviva. Somehow I think all of this must be a bad dream."

"You want to hear about a bad dream?" Yitzy asked, thinking about his dream of being trapped in a computer game.

"Tell me about it on our way to Rabbi Lantzman," his father answered.

* * * *

When Rabbi Lantzman arrived home, he found the computer investigator Mr. Hall sitting in his living room. Mr. Hall stood up to greet him. "Rabbi Lantzman, my name is Hall. I'm with the Network Security Agency," he said, showing the rabbi a badge and an identification card. "Your wife was kind enough to let me wait here for you to return. I'm examining some interference with the National Computer Network, NatNet." Mr. Hall sat down again and continued, "I was hoping you would be able to help me."

The rabbi was surprised at Mr. Hall's request. "I'm afraid I don't know anything about your network," he said. "Are you sure you have the right person?"

Mr. Hall, paying no attention to the rabbi's answer, opened his briefcase and pulled out a folder. "I believe you have had occasion to work with one Yitzy Berg, the son of

Shlomo Berg of the Software Center. Is that true?"

From the tone of the question, the rabbi suddenly began to realize he was under investigation, but for what? "I know Yitzy, of course. He's one of my students."

"A student, then," said Mr. Hall. "Makes sense. One of those college kids out to prove how much he knows about computers. They do it all the time, you know. Wreck a computer system and then try to get jobs based on how well they know how to break the computer."

Rabbi Lantzman had to laugh. "No," he said, "Yitzy's not it college."

"Not in college?" Mr. Hall asked. "You mean he's one those computer punks who get their kicks breaking the computers. Juvenile delinquents. They should stick to putting toothpaste in parking meters and soaping car windows."

"I'm afraid Yitzy's not even in high school," Rabbi Lantzman offered. "He's in my seventh grade class."

Mr. Hall turned red at this. "You mean a lousy seventh grader has brought the NatNet to its knees? I hate it when these kids are given access to systems they know nothing about, start messing around, and bring the whole system down. Was it you that gave him access to the network?"

"I told you, already, Mr. Hall, I don't know anything about the network," said Rabbi Lantzman.

"Well, someone must have put him on there. His father says he had nothing to do with it either, but here are the records of his intrusions," said Mr. Hall, handing over the folder to Rabbi Lantzman.

The rabbi looked over the papers in the folder. They contained several reports that described mysterious files appearing on computer systems all over the country. "But these files," the rabbi said with surprise, "they contained Yitzy's essay. How in the world did it get from the school to computers all over the country?"

Mr. Hall grabbed the folder back. "So you know about the files," he said angrily. "You just said you didn't know anything about them."

"What I tried to explain ..." the rabbi began and then stopped. *Could this have anything to do with Yitzy's use of the G.O.L.E.M.*, he thought? *But how could his files get to a network?*

"I realize you are a rabbi," said Mr. Hall, "but I want you to know, we are treating this violation of the network very seriously. If you or anyone you know was involved, we expect you to come forward voluntarily. If not, well, we have a way to get at the truth."

"I was just thinking about Yitzy's access to the school's computer," said the rabbi, wondering what Mr. Hall would do if he didn't get the information he needed. "But I don't see how he could use that computer to get to your network. Maybe we should speak to Yitzy himself."

Mr. Hall put the folder back in his briefcase. "I've sent one of my assistants to do just that. Until he reports, I would like some more information about the school computer you mentioned."

Just after Yitzy and Dr. Berg left, Mrs. Berg heard a knock at the door. When she looked out the small window in the door she saw the back of what looked like a refrigerator in a business suit. The fridge turned around and then she saw a badge in its hand. "Are you a policeman?" she asked, in a frightened tone.

"Mrs. Berg," she heard through the door, "my name is Peters. I'm not a policeman, but I am a federal investigator. I'm looking into some computer network problems. Can I come in and talk to you and your family for a few minutes?"

Mrs. Berg opened the door slowly. "Normally, I wouldn't let in a, .." she paused for a minute, "a stranger without some warning. But I know what you are investigating."

Peters started to laugh. "I know what you're thinking. My appearance comes in handy. You'd be surprised how many crooks take one look at me and suddenly feel guilty."

Mrs. Berg started to smile. "I don't know too much about the computer problems. You probably want to talk to my husband." Mrs. Berg explained that he and her son were on their way to Rabbi Lantzman's.

"Rabbi Lantzman," he repeated. "That's where my partner is. I've got to let him know that this might be some kind of conspiracy. May I use your phone?"

Mrs. Berg showed Peters to the phone as he checked the number in his notebook. He called and asked for his partner. "That's right. They're on their way over," Peters said to Hall, not realizing Mrs. Berg could overhear him. "Do you want to call for a back-up? They may be planning some new twist on this. Maybe we should arrest them all right there." Just then Peters heard a thump.

"Say, Hall," he said as he looked around to find the cause of the noise, "when you call for the back-up, send a paramedic over here." He listened to Hall's answer. "No, not for me, the kid's mother just fainted."

Chapter 15

Spin Control

Yitzy and his father found Rabbi Lantzman and Mr. Hall waiting for them at the rabbi's house. Dr. Berg was surprised that Mr. Hall seemed to be expecting them, not knowing Hall had just gotten off the phone with Peters.

"Dr. Berg," Hall greeted them as they entered the Lantzmans house, "we've been expecting you. And this must be little Yitzy. Glad to finally meet the juvenile delinquent who's netted up the knotnat. I mean, natted up the net knot."

Yitzy and his father started to laugh at Mr. Hall's slip. "Knotted up the Natnet," Mr. Hall corrected himself, "and this is no laughing matter. All of you may have to pay for Yitzy's little prank on his computer."

"Now, just a minute, Hall," Dr. Berg said, getting upset.

"We're trying to solve a problem here, not assign guilt. And I really think it's foolish to blame this problem on a twelve year old."

"Dr. Berg," Hall said, also getting angry, "the good rabbi and I have just been discussing some of the computer antics of your little angel. He hardly seems like the innocent youth you seem to think he is."

Is this some kind of a tennis match? Yitzy thought, watching the arguments flying back and forth. "I didn't mean any harm," he said. "I've already told my father and Rabbi Lantzman everything that happened. What else can I do?"

"You can sit there and be quiet and don't cause any more harm, until we settle this," Hall ordered.

Dr. Berg stood up. "You're way out of line, Hall," he said quietly. We came over here to help, not to be accused of crimes we didn't commit."

Hall calmed himself down, realizing he might ruin his case if he made improper statements to his suspects. "We'll see who gets accused and what they did commit," Hall said smartly. "I've already called for some additional personnel to help with this case. So just sit tight for a few minutes."

Suddenly, the room grew quiet. Everyone sensed that Hall had plans for more than a discussion and didn't want to start up with him again.

The ringing of the phone broke the quiet. "I'll get that," said Hall jumping for the phone.

"Hall here," he said. Not knowing what was happening, the three suspects watched him nod as he listened to the other end. "Who said they're sending a crew over here?" he said finally. "You mean the TV stations? How did they get wind of this?"

"We're gonna be on TV?" Yitzy whispered to his father.

"It sounds like Hall will do what he can to prevent that," his father answered. "Say, Rabbi Lantzman, what's the story about Yitzy's work on the school computer. As he described it, there's no way I can figure he could get to the Natnet."

Rabbi Lantzman thought again about Yitzy's actions on the computer. "He may have sent some data to the Kessernet, you know the Jewish bulletin service."

"I've used that myself," said Dr. Berg. "But sending data wouldn't unleash a virus. He would have to run a program on the Kessernet computer to start the virus."

Mr. Hall had hung up and now addressed Dr. Berg. "We've got some more information on the source of the virus that might interest you. It came from a computer in New York called, let me check here," he said looking at his notebook, "called Kessernet. Ever hear of it?"

Without an answer, Mr. Hall realized he had just set off a bomb. "Judging by your looks," he said. "You may have just all confessed to mail fraud and systems tampering. Now, all we need to determine is which of you is Golem."

"G.O.L.E.M.," Yitzy yelled out. "That was the name of the program I was running when all this happened."

"I see what you're thinking, Hall," said Dr. Berg, interrupting his son. "But I've got another suggestion."

"I'd be glad to listen to it, Dr. Berg," Hall answered. "But don't count on its changing my mind."

Dr. Berg then stated his case: What if there was a real network cracker on Kessernet who just happened to get copies of our files as he set off the virus. "Then the virus would carry the files," he said. "It was just coincidence that our files got in there."

"And I'm descended from the Ten Lost Tribes," Hall laughed. "Let's get serious. One of you started a virus, maybe the others are innocent, but there's too much going on between you to eliminate that explanation."

"I think Dr. Berg has a point," said Rabbi Lantzman. "It's possible that the cracker used the Kessernet as a gateway into the Natnet. And it would make sense for a cracker to use Kessernet on Friday night when the traffic is low and no one is monitoring it."

"And what does Friday night have to do with anything?" asked Hall, sarcastically.

"That's when the virus was let loose," entered Dr. Berg. "And Friday night is the Jewish Sabbath when there aren't many users of Kessernet."

Mr. Hall looked embarrassed. "I forgot about Friday night being your Sabbath. Let me apologize for that. But you still admit to copying files into the network through Kessernet. You have to assume responsibility."

"Yeah, Ta," said Yitzy. "We should have kept our sheep locked up."

"One more word about sheep!" muttered Hall.

"You're right, Yitzy," said Dr. Berg. "You shouldn't have used my disk to copy your file to, and I shouldn't have used the disk after you used it. But Mr. Golem in New York didn't keep his sheep locked up, either. Somehow, he let our files get into his virus before he shipped it all over the network."

"Like it says in the *Gemara*," Yitzy added, "it happened while he was asleep."

"What do you mean, Yitzy?" his father asked.

"It says at the end of the *Gemara*," Yitzy explained, "we're responsible even when we're asleep. He didn't even know the file was there when he let his program loose."

"That's it," said Dr. Berg. "He must have planned to monitor the progress of his virus, by looking at the network."

"Sort of like an arsonist returning to the scene of the fire he set," said Hall.

"Exactly," said Rabbi Lantzman. "He fell asleep at the terminal and can't possibly know what's actually happening with the extra files. But how would he monitor the network?" the rabbi asked Yitzy's father.

"Probably the same way he started the virus," said Dr. Berg, "through the Kessernet."

"But if he was asleep," said Yitzy, "he's certainly awake by now. Won't he know he's still connected to the system?"

"Maybe he fell asleep while he was monitoring it," answered Yitzy's father. "He may not know he's still logged in. I've done that myself when I've dialed into the work computer from home and left my terminal running. Sometimes I won't catch it for a day or two. If he is still connected, we can trace him from Kessernet back to his home computer."

Mr. Hall was taking this all in. "It's starting to make sense now," he said. "Let me call into the S.W.A.T. center to see if they've made any progress on the New York connection and tell them what we know. By the way, do you have a computer here?"

Rabbi Lantzman answered that he didn't have one, but there was one at the school, a few blocks away.

"Let's head over there and check the Kessernet," said

Hall. "And hurry, we want to get out of here before the press shows up."

Chapter 16

Unchained

The office was stiflingly hot when the foursome, Mr. Hall, Rabbi Lantzman, Yitzy and his father, entered the room housing the computer. Had it been only two days since Yitzy had found himself trying to unchain himself from the G.O.L.E.M.? Yet here he was again, using the computer to undo the damage he had caused, or at least contributed to. His dream was coming true, he really was trapped in a computer game.

"Let me get started here by accessing the Kessernet," said Rabbi Lantzman, entering the phone number through the modem. "I hope I don't get a busy signal."

"Don't worry about that," said Hall. "We have ways to clear the phone lines if you need it."

"You have ways to do just about everything," said Yitzy with a smile.

"The kid's finally catching on," Hall said proudly.

"There it is," said the Rabbi. "I'm logged in."

"Can you check for the users?" asked Dr. Berg.

Rabbi Lantzman entered a few commands and a list appeared showing the user identifications. They quickly read through the list:

lantzman	3	0:	00:	02
levi	7	0:	02:	10
golem	4	1:	22:	31
berger	1	0:	01:	24

"There it is!" shouted Yitzy.

"What are the numbers after the names?" asked Mr. Hall.

"The first number shows the telephone line each user is attached to," said Rabbi Lantzman. "The next number is the time each user has been connected. You see, I've been on about two minutes, but our friend the Golem, one day twenty-two hours."

"He's been on since he let the virus loose," observed Dr. Berg. "He must have walked away, forgetting he was still logged in. But how can we get to him?"

Mr. Hall headed for a phone he saw in the outer office. "If we can get the phone number that Golem's connected to, I can trace back to the number he's calling from."

"You have ways to do that too?" asked Yitzy. "Figures."

"Just get to the Kessernet operator, and we'll trace it all right. Do whatever you have to, but get that number," said Hall. "In the meantime, I'm checking back with the S.W.A.T. team to fill them in."

Rabbi Lantzman sent a message to the system operator, but there was no way of knowing if he would be available.

It was just luck to find him watching the system at any given hour of the day. They waited silently for a few minutes to see if the operator would respond.

"What if you can't reach him?" asked Dr. Berg, breaking the silence.

"I have some phone numbers to try," said Rabbi Lantzman. "I know some of the people who run the system. All they need to do is give me the incoming phone numbers."

"That's right," said Hall, as he spoke to the S.W.A.T. Center on the other end of the phone he held. "We can run a trace on all of them."

They directed their attention back to the terminal, waiting for a reply. Rabbi Lantzman was getting no response to his messages to the operator and he entered a command to get important phone numbers. "I'll call one of the operators I know. Say, Hall, what do you hear from the S.W.A.T. Center?"

"They've analyzed the virus and are sending out information on how to eliminate it," he said. "Finding this Golem culprit will be icing on the cake."

"How do they solve these problems so fast?" wondered Yitzy.

"When you have so many systems linked," answered his father, "it's easy to do a lot of damage quickly, but it's also easy to correct it. All of the users can work together to solve the problem and then help each other fix it."

"Do you think your work will still be blamed for the problems?" Yitzy asked.

"Well, we have a great public relations guy," answered his father. "He'll put a positive spin on it."

Rabbi Lantzman was busy writing down the phone

numbers of the Kessernet operators. He was ready to try calling each of them, if he didn't get a computer message back.

"What's a positive spin?" asked Yitzy, after thinking about his father's answer for a few minutes..

"That means he'll turn what looked like a disaster into something like a major victory," said Hall sarcastically. "Like they planned it that way all along."

"Hey," said Yitzy, "*gam zu l-tovah*," referring to the concept from the Talmud of finding a happy side to even the most frightful events.

"What did he say?" said Hall.

Rabbi Lantzman tried to explain it to Hall. "It's Hebrew for positive spin. Are you off the phone yet?" he asked. "I have some numbers to call, too."

There wasn't much else that had happened at the center. "As soon as you have the numbers coming into Kessernet, let me know. I want to get the traces started."

Rabbi Lantzman tried two of the numbers without luck. With each passing minute, the possibility increased that the Golem in New York would "wake up" and discover what was happening. It was critical that they reach an operator. Rabbi Lantzman finally reached one of the system operators and got the Golem's line number. "I've got the number that Golem's using," he shouted for joy.

Hall took the number and phoned an office in New York to get the trace started. "They'll have the number in minutes, just wait."

As everyone in the room waited for the phone to ring back with the information on the trace, they heard a sudden rush of noise outside the office. Suddenly, Peters burst in the door. "They followed me over here from the rabbi's house," he said. "I'll do what I can to hold them back."

"What are you talking about?" yelled Hall.

"The TV cameras," said Peters. "There are a dozen reporters out here trying to find out what's going on."

Yitzy ran to the window to see four remote TV vans with satellite dishes on towers pointing out above them. He also saw cars with the names of newspapers on them. "They're here all right," he reported. "Looks like every TV station in Pittsburgh."

"Keep them out of here," yelled Hall. "Can you phone the police?" he said to Rabbi Lantzman "they're trespassing if they come inside."

"I thought you already had the police on the way," said the rabbi.

"I did?" said Hall with some embarrassment. "Oh that, well, uh, to be honest, I never had any plans to arrest you. Not today at least. I was just hoping to get you to admit what you were up to. I wish now I had called them, though."

"I have a confession to make, too," said Dr. Berg. "I just made up that whole story about the Golem still being logged in. I was just stalling for time and nearly fainted when his name showed up in the list of users."

"Why you little..." Mr. Hall blew up just as the phone rang and they all jumped for it. Hall grabbed it first. "You've got his name and address? Great," he said. "Is there someone on the way over to check it out?" He paused for a second while the other three looked on. "Gentleman, we have the Golem."

"Mr. Hall, can we wrap it up here and go home?" asked

Rabbi Lantzman.

"Just don't leave town any time soon," Hall answered. "We'll be needing to take formal statements."

"Well, Yitzy," Rabbi Lantzman asked, "are you ready to meet the press?"

* * * *

Outside the school, Peters was doing his best at crowd control. A police car arrived, and two uniformed officers stepped out to help direct traffic around the gathering crowd. In all, there were reporters and photographers from three newspapers, four television stations, and a number of radio stations.

"Now, here are the rules," Peters told the press. "Mr. Hall, chief investigator of the Network Security Agency will make a brief statement. Each of you will be allowed to ask him two questions."

"Will we be able to direct questions to the civilians?" called one of the reporters.

"That's their call, and you just used up one of your questions," he answered as the other reporters laughed. Mr. Hall, Rabbi Lantzman, Dr. Berg and Yitzy emerged from the yeshiva to the glare of TV lights and the clicking of the photographers' cameras. "Now I'd like to introduce Mr. Hall."

"Thanks, Peters," Hall began. "You are all aware that over the past 48 hours we have faced a serious attack on our major national computer system, the NatNet. A virus was released, attacking computers all over the country. While it appeared that there was a negative Pittsburgh connection impacting on our computing resources ..."

"What did he say?" Yitzy whispered to his father.

"He's saying he thought we were guilty," Dr. Berg answered.

"... it has now been confirmed that the Pittsburgh connection was purely coincidental," Hall continued. "In fact, that connection may have led to the quick solution of the case. Together with the S.W.A.T. at the Pittsburgh Computer Center, Rabbi Lantzman, Dr. Berg and his son have been instrumental in supporting our investigation. In that connection, I have been authorized to announce that we have apprehended a suspect in New York."

The crowd suddenly became noisy and several of the newspaper reporters ran back to their cars to phone in the late-breaking story. "Can you tell us any specifics about him?" a reporter called out, as Peters glared back at her.

"I cannot give any more details about the suspect," Hall answered. "Only that he used the code-name "Golem," that's G-o-l-e-m, and that when he was arrested the N.Y.P.D. found in his possession significant evidence of related criminal activity. I'm afraid that's all the details I can give you about our suspect. I would be happy to answer a few background questions."

The reporters began quizzing Hall on the methods used to track down Golem, and Yitzy and his father agreed that Hall gave them a lot of credit. "He seemed pretty mean at first," Yitzy said, "but he's okay."

"I wish I could say the same for Peters," said Yitzy's father.

Just then Mrs. Berg arrived. She had trouble getting through the crowds until Peters spotted her. Suddenly, a passage was opened in front of her.

"Oh, Yitzy," she said, giving her son a big hug. Mr. Hall was no longer the center of attention as the cameras turned to catch the reunion between mother and son.

"Are you all right?" Dr. Berg asked his wife.

"I've recovered," she answered looking sternly at Peters who seemed to shrink in his shoes at her stare. "I had recovered on my own before the paramedics arrived."

"Paramedics?" Dr. Berg asked bewildered. "What are you talking about."

Mrs. Berg glared back at Peters again, and caught him looking at her with a slightly apologetic glance. "That, that man," she said, pointing at Peters, "told someone he was prepared to arrest you and Yitzy." She went on the explain how she had fainted for a second, but had quickly revived herself. "And then Peters ran out of the house without even an explanation or an apology."

"I'm about to faint, too," Yitzy said. "Can we go home, now? I'm awfully hungry."

Just then, one of the TV reporters came over to them. "Are you the author of the article that appeared on the sports page today?" she asked.

Yitzy looked around, not knowing what she was talking about. *What did I do now*, he wondered.

"In all the excitement," Mrs. Berg laughed, "we forgot to tell you. Somehow the file that was sent around the network, the one containing your report, got copied into an article in the sports page."

"Wow," Yitzy said, "that's even better than the school newsletter."

The reporter asked if she could get some pictures of the

family as a photographer flashed away. "I'd like to ask you some questions about the case, Dr. Berg," the reporter said.

Dr. Berg held up his hand and explained that he did not want to answer any questions. "Because of the involvement of the N.S.A. and the Computer Center, I would like you to direct your questions through official channels."

They then turned to Yitzy, and asked him about his background in computers and about his involvement. He looked questioningly at his father. "Well, I use the computer to do homework and play games," he said.

"How did you get involved in this network mess-up?" someone asked him.

"Can I say, no comment?" Yitzy asked.

"You certainly may," his father told him.

"Did you learn anything from your involvement?" another reporter asked."Yes ," said Yitzy decisively. "Jewish law, which is thousands of years old, teachers that a farmer is responsible to keep his sheep and cattle from damaging someone else's belongings. I learned that these laws are always important even now in the computer age; we need to keep stuff like a runaway virus from destroying someone else's property."

"Well said!" exclaimed Dr. Berg with a tired smile. "Let's go."

"Under the circumstances," Rabbi Lantzman said as Yitzy started to leave, "I think I'll excuse you from your job here tomorrow."

Yitzy had almost forgotten about his "community service" punishment. "Rabbi Lantzman," he asked, "can I still do my *tshuva*?"

"What are you talking about, Yitzy?" his mother asked.

Rabbi Lantzman jumped in before Yitzy could answer. "Yitzy just wants to make amends for some of things he did. You don't mind?" asked the Rabbi.

"Mind? it sounds like a very good idea to me," she said, giving her son a proud hug. "Let's go home."

Chapter 17

Tshuvah

Yitzy got to school the next morning shortly after ten. The phone had rung non-stop the night before and Yitzy was still tired. All his friends wanted to ask him about his adventure.

Memorial Day was one of the few secular holidays on which the school closed, so he missed what could have been a full day off. To add to that he was missing the big baseball game. But Rabbi Lantzman was right: he was already feeling positive about having a specific way to make up for his big mistake.

He arrived at the office, expecting to find Rabbi Lantzman there. Instead, Mrs. McKay came out to greet him. "Why, hello, Yitzy," she said. "You're a real celebrity today. I was so happy to hear you had volunteered to help us with the graduation mailing for the Girls' Division."

115

Oh, no, thought Yitzy, *I thought I was doing community service, not hard labor. What am I going to do for her?*

"With the graduation coming up," Mrs. McKay explained, "we must notify all the parents and anyone else involved with the school of our lovely plans for that special event. We have one girl reciting a simply beautiful poem by Miss Emily Dickinson. You know of her, of course, from our poetry lesson last week. And then there's another graduate who will be reading her essay. It's going to be a marvelous evening."

One I'll be sure to miss, Yitzy said to himself.

"Well, let's get started," she said. Mrs. McKay went on in her usual manner, describing how Yitzy had to carefully fold all the graduation announcements, place them in envelopes, seal them and then address them. "We have mailing labels for you to place on the envelopes. Then you can sort them."

"How do I sort them, Mrs. McKay?" Yitzy asked.

Mrs. McKay explained about the sorting procedure and Yitzy started his task. "Now, be very careful. We don't want any of the invitations to be creased, do we?"

Oh, brother, thought Yitzy, *this is going to be hard labor.* Luckily, after about fifteen minutes, Mrs. McKay said she had some other things to work on. "But I'll be back to check on you," she said as she left the office.

"Don't hurry on my account," Yitzy thought, as he continued with his work. Actually, it wasn't too bad. Although it was very hot outside, someone had turned on the air conditioner in the office, so he was at least spared the awful heat that usually filled the building. But the time passed so slowly.

As noon approached, he had finished most of the folding, and he sat down to eat the snack he had brought from home. After his snack, Yitzy started working on the invitations again. He had been folding for another hour or so, when Rabbi Lantzman walked in. The rabbi was dressed for the baseball game Yitzy had been missing. "Good to see you so hard at work," he said to Yitzy.

"Well," Yitzy said, "I'm learning a lot about the cost of not locking my sheep up properly." Rabbi Lantzman smiled at that. "How's the game going?" Yitzy asked.

"It's a close one," Rabbi Lantzman answered. "If you leave now, you might even make the last inning or two."

"I've still got tons of work here, though," Yitzy replied. "Putting the invitations in the envelopes, addressing, sorting. What fun."

"I think that can wait until tomorrow," the rabbi said.

"You mean it?" Yitzy asked.

"Sure, even the convicts at Leavenworth have recreation time. We'll see you tomorrow after school, okay?"

"You bet," he said. "Thanks, Rabbi Lantzman, you're the greatest."

Yitzy bolted out of the office, down the stairs and out to his bicycle. He was just a short drive away from the game - down Murray to Solway and a block over to Wightman Field. He glanced up at the office window as he left the school, and saw Rabbi Lantzman looking down. Yitzy had a big smile on his face as he waved to his favorite teacher. If he hurried, he could be at the game in just a few minutes.

Chapter 18

The Final Inning

Yitzy's ride to the park must have set a speed record. In spite of the holiday, there was plenty of traffic around Squirrel Hill, and he had to dart between cars and pedestrians.

By the time he got to the game, he was soaked with perspiration from the ride in the heat, but he was happy to be joining his friends. "Hey, Yitzy," Moishy called to him as he saw him get off his bike and go toward the field. "What are you doing here? I thought it was community service day."

"Watch it, Moishy," Yitzy warned him. "Do you want the whole world to know? Rabbi Lantzman let me go early so I could watch part of the game. What inning is it, anyway?"

"We're heading into the top of the ninth, and we're behind 3-2," Moishy answered.

Suddenly, some of the players and fans noticed Yitzy had

arrived. A small crowd gathered around him. "Can I have your autograph?" laughed Chaim.

"When are you to be on Nightline?" asked Yitzy's friend Shmuli.

"Cut it out," Yitzy said bashfully. "Have any of you played at all? "Yitzy wondered.

"Are you kidding?" Moishy grimaced. "But I'm rooting for the high school boys, anyway."

Moishy and Yitzy joined the rest of their classmates in the bleachers along the first base line to watch the game.

"Say, I have to go talk to Joe," Yitzy said to his friends. "I'll be back in a minute."

Joe was coaching the "Sons" team and was standing behind their bench. He was watching the "Fathers" team bat in their half of the ninth. There was already one out as Yitzy called to him.

"Hi, Yitzy," Joe said happily. "I wasn't sure whether you'd ever make it. Now that you're famous, you'll forget all your old friends."

Yitzy gathered up whatever courage he had left and started his apology to Joe. "I'm sorry that you were so embarrassed on *Shabbos*."

"Me, embarrassed?" Joe laughed. "If you want to hear about embarrassment, I could tell you a dozen stories about myself. Make that five or six," Joe corrected himself, "the rest I couldn't tell a twelve year old."

"Well, it was my fault that the announcements were all messed up," Yitzy explained.

Joe nodded at Yitzy's explanation. "You did that too?" Joe said with a laugh. "You're about the fifth person to tell me it was all their fault. I thought the purpose of the computer was to save on labor, not spread it around."

Yitzy started to tell him the whole story about the newsletter, and the computer game, and how he had gotten into the G.O.L.E.M. program when Joe interrupted him. "If you think I'm going learn about computers at my age," Joe said, "you're going to be very disappointed. All I know is, if Rabbi Lantzman gave you instructions that you didn't follow, you better correct yourself in the future. But about the embarrassment, I've never had so much fun making the announcements. You should have seen Mr. Greenberg's face when I made that remark about his first wife. You wouldn't ..."

Joe noticed that the "Fathers" had made their last out. The "Sons" were coming to bat in the bottom of the ninth, trailing by a run. "With your brother coming up fourth," Joe said, "we've got some real power. But someone's got to get on to give him a chance."

The first two batters hit lazy ground balls to the infield. Then Shuie Friedman was up. Shuie hit a solid single to left and stretched it to a double. With two outs, Dovid came to bat, needing a hit to tie the score.

"What happens if the inning ends in a tie?" Yitzy asked. "Do we go to extra innings?"

Joe looked at his watch. "No," he answered "I'm afraid this will be the final inning. There's another game starting at two, so we have to be off the field by then. Come on, Dovid, send us home with a homer," Joe called.

Dovid stood at the plate and watched two pitches go by. On the third pitch, he took a hefty swing and launched a fly ball deep to center, beyond the running outfielder's outstretched glove. But as he left the batters box, Dovid seemed to stumble and had to limp to first on what could have been the game-winning home run.

Joe ran over to talk to him. "Are you okay?" Joe asked.

"I just twisted my ankle," Dovid answered. "Let me try to walk it off."

Joe called for time, while Dovid tried to work out the pain in his ankle, but he could barely walk, let alone run. "You better send in someone to run for me," Dovid said.

Joe looked at Yitzy. "Get in there and run for your brother," Joe said. "That way, I won't have to change the name on the scorecard. Berg running for Berg," he called to the other bench.

Yitzy took his place on first, and with two outs he knew he had to run on anything the next batter hit. Dovid's hit had scored the tying run. Now it was up to Yitzy to score the winning run. Yitzy concentrated on the pitcher, then he looked down to home as Ari Goldman stepped into the batter's box. Ari was another power hitter, so Yitzy could easily score from first on an extra base hit.

Ari stood in the batter's box, waiting for his pitch. He took the first pitch, a ball outside and low. He fouled off the next two pitches down the right field line. Now the count stood at one ball and two strikes and all the attention was on Ari and Yitzy, who was still on first.

Ari swung and connected with the next pitch. Yitzy was off with the pitch and was almost to second when he saw Ari's hit turning foul again. "Straighten it out, Ari," Joe called to him. And everyone on the home team bench and in the bleachers was on their feet, waiting for the deciding pitch.

Ari waited, and timed this pitch perfectly. When it came,

he belted a drive between right and center. Yitzy was off. He charged toward second, but even at top speed it felt like he was climbing a steep hill. As he rounded second and headed for third the hill got even steeper. *It's just like my dream coming back again*, Yitzy thought. Every corner he turned, the climb became harder and harder. He was now rounding third, and he could hear the cheers of his team-mates as he approached home coming in to score. The hill felt even steeper now and Yitzy could see a boulder head-ing down towards him. No, it was the throw from the out-field, he realized. He had to slide to avoid the tag, and hope the ball was thrown off the mark.

Yitzy slid into home in a head-first dive. He saw the catcher waiting for the throw and he didn't know if he had been tagged out or not. Then he was mobbed by his cheer-ing team and classmates and he knew.

"Yitzy did it," they shouted. "He won the game for us."

Yitzy got up slowly and brushed himself off, as everyone crowded around. Then, he heard them start up the familiar chant, "Yitz Berg, from Pittsburgh. Yitz Berg, from Pitts-burgh," but now, with a warm feeling of belonging, Yitzy could smile along with all of them.

Next Volume in this Series

Available Soon at Your Local Bookstore